Conrad Ferdinand Meyer, Sarah Holland Adams

The Monk's Wedding

a novel

Conrad Ferdinand Meyer, Sarah Holland Adams

The Monk's Wedding
a novel

ISBN/EAN: 9783337351182

Printed in Europe, USA, Canada, Australia, Japan

Cover: Foto ©Andreas Hilbeck / pixelio.de

More available books at **www.hansebooks.com**

THE MONK'S WEDDING

A NOVEL

BY

Conrad Ferdinand Meyer

BOSTON
CUPPLES AND HURD
94 Boylston Street
1887

THE MONK'S WEDDING.

It was evening in Verona. Round a
spacious hearth, glowing with a fire which
filled its roomy depth and centre, sat a
princely group. In the centre — Lord and
Master — was that Scaliger whom they
called Cangrande. Of the blooming ladies
on either side of him, the one nearest to the
fire and half in shadow, was his wife; the
other upon whom the full light shone, his
relative and friend. Near them were the
other members of the party, leaving the
remainder of the hearth free, according to
courtly custom, and with significant glances
and half-suppressed laughter they were telling stories.

Into this brilliant, joyous company, a grave
man entered, whose stern features and long
flowing robe seemed out of another world.

"Prince, I come to warm myself at your
hearth," said the stranger, in a tone of

mingled seriousness and disdain, adding reproachfully, " The negligent servants, despite
this frosty evening, have delayed, or forgotten, to light the fire in the upper guest-
chamber."

"Take a seat beside me, my Dante," replied Cangrande, "but, if you would feel a
genial warmth, you must not sit, as is your
wont, mutely gazing at the flames.   We are
amusing each other with stories and the hand
which has to-day forged the Terza Rima (for
in my astrological chamber I overheard you
scanning the verse,) this mighty hand, I say,
must consent to grasp our diverting plaything
without shivering it to pieces.   Dismiss the
Goddesses " — he meant the Muses — "for a
while and satisfy yourself with these lovely
mortals " — and with a graceful wave of the
hand Cangrande directed the eyes of his
guest to the two ladies.   Seemingly unconscious of his presence, the taller of them had
not thought of moving, whilst the younger
and more sprightly one gladly made place
for the Florentine beside her.   Disregard-
ing, however, the invitation of his host he
proudly chose a seat at the end of the table.

Either he was displeased at finding two ladies at the side of the Prince, if only for an evening, or he was disgusted with the court-fool who, with legs stretched out before him, was sitting on Cangrande's mantle which had fallen to the ground.

This fool, a toothless old man, with goggle eyes and soft sensual mouth, fit only for gabbling and licking sweet-meats, was beside Dante, the one elderly man in the company. He was called Gocciola, which means " little drop "— because it was his habit to secretly collect the little drops clinging to the empty glasses. He hated the Florentine with a kind of childish spite, seeing in him a rival for the, not always daintily bestowed, favor of the Prince. He made up a face, and grinning scornfully, had the boldness to call the attention of his pretty neighbor on the left to the profile of the poet sharply outlined upon the ceiling of the lofty room. Dante's profile was like that of a gigantic woman, with long aquiline nose and drooping lips — one of the Parcæ — or weird sisters. The light-hearted maiden turned aside to hide a childlike laugh. A clever looking youth,

who now drew nearer and was named Ascanio, helped her to smother it by addressing
Dante with that measure of reverence with
which the poet liked to be approached.

"Thou who art Italy's Homer and Virgil"
— he said — "I beg of thee scorn not to
share in our innocent sport. Deign to en-
tertain us tonight, not with song, but with
story."

"What is your theme?" Dante asked,
still harshly though somewhat less ungra-
ciously than at first.

"Sudden change of profession, with good,
bad, or laughable results." the youth replied
quickly. Dante was silent for a moment;
with melancholy eyes he thoughtfully sur-
veyed the company which did not wholly dis-
please him, for he discovered, together with
many shallow brows, some that were strik-
ingly noble and powerful. "Has any one
of you made the uncowling of a monk his
theme?" he enquired, already in a milder
tone.

"Yes, Dante," answered a soldier with a
slightly foreign accent, who was dressed in
chain armor, had an earnest, good-natured

face, and wore a long drooping moustache. "I have related the story of the young Manuccio who leapt over the walls of his cloister to become a soldier."

"He did right," responded Dante, "for he had deceived himself as to his calling."

A pert and somewhat voluptuous Paduan, named Tsotta, now interrupted with — "Master, I have narrated the story of Helena Manenta, who after her first curl had fallen under the consecrated shears covered the rest with both hands and slurred over her nun's vows, for among the people in the nave of the church she had caught sight of her lover who was carried off into slavery, but had been miraculously released, and was now hanging up his chains "— she was going to say — "in the church," when Dante cut short her chatter by saying, "And she also did well for she acted out the instincts of her amorous nature, but I shall tell you of a wholly different case from any that has been here mentioned. There was a monk who, not from his own instinct, nor from any longing for, worldly pleasure, or power, nor because he had mistaken the bent of his capacities

or talents, but for the love of another, under
the compulsion of another's will, on the
ground of what may indeed be called filial
piety, became false to himself; broke vows
made to himself even more than to the
church; flung aside the rope and cowl which
had never been a trial to him, but on the
contrary, had seemed a part of himself. Has
this been related? No? Good! Then I will
do it; but, my patron and protector, say
what must be the end of such a thing?" —
and he turned to Cangrande.

"It must necessarily be bad," he replied
without hesitation — "Who voluntarily takes
a leap, leaps well; — who is pushed to it
leaps badly."

"Thou speakest the truth, Prince," responded Dante, "for if I understand it, the
Apostle meant just this when writing to the
Romans, that 'whatever is not of faith is sin,'
which means acting against the truth of
nature, and our highest convictions."

"Is it at all necessary that there should
be monks?" whispered a voice out of a dim
corner, as if to suggest that any sort of
escape from an unnatural condition was a
blessing.

The audacious question caused no shock, for at this court the boldest discussion of religious matters was allowed, yes, smiled upon, whilst a free or incautious word in regard to the person or policy of the Emperor was certain destruction.

Dante's eyes sought the speaker and recognized in him a young ecclesiastic whose fingers toyed with the heavy gold cross he · wore over his priestly robe.

" Not on my account," said the Florentine deliberately, " May the monks die out as soon as a race is born that understands how to unite justice and mercy — the two highest attributes of the human soul — which seem now to exclude one another. Until that late hour in the world's history may the State administer the one, and the church the other. Since, however, the exercise of mercy requires a thoroughly unselfish heart, the three monastic vows are not only a proper but essential preparation ; for experience has taught that total abnegation is less difficult than a reserved and partial self-surrender."

" Are there not more bad than good monks ? " persisted the doubting ecclesiastic.

"No," said Dante, "when we take into consideration human weakness; else there are more unjust than righteous judges, more cowards than brave warriors, more bad men than good."

"And is not this the case?" asked the guest in the dim corner. "No, certainly not," Dante replied, a heavenly brightness suddenly illuminating his stern features. "Is not philosophy asking and striving to to find out how evil came into this world? Had the bad formed the majority we should, on the contrary, have been asking how good came into the world."

This proud enigmatical remark impressed the party forcibly but at the same time excited some apprehension lest the Florentine was going deeper into scholasticism instead of relating his story.

Cangrande saw his pretty young friend suppress a yawn, and said "Noble Dante, are you to tell us a true story or will you embellish a legend current among the people; or can you not give us a pure invention of your own laurel-crowned head?"

Dante replied with slow emphasis, "I evolve my story from an inscription on a grave."

"On a grave!"

"Yes, from an inscription on a grave stone which I read years ago when with the Franciscans at Padua. The stone was in a corner of the cloister garden hidden under wild rose bushes, but still accessible to the novices, if they crept on all fours and did not mind scratching their cheeks with thorns. I ordered the prior, or I should say, besought him, to have the puzzling stone removed to the library, and there commended to the interest of a gray-headed custodian.

"What was on the stone?" interposed somewhat listlessly the wife of the Prince.

"The inscription," answered Dante, "was in Latin and ran thus:—

"Hic jacet monachus Astorre cum uxore Antiope. Sepeliebat Azzolinus.'"

"What does it mean?" eagerly cried the lady on Cangrande's left.

The Prince fluently translated:—

"Here sleeps the monk Astorre beside his wife Antiope. Both buried by Ezzelin."

"Atrocious tyrant!" exclaimed the impressible maiden, "I am sure he had them buried alive, because they were lovers, — and he insulted the poor victims, even in their graves, by styling her the 'wife of the monk', — cruel wretch that he was!"

" Hardly, " said Dante, " I construe it quite differently, and according to the history this seems improbable; for Ezzelin's rigor was directed rather against breaches of ecclesiastical discipline. He interested himself little either in the making or breaking of sacred vows. I take the 'Sepeliebat' in a friendly sense, and believe the meaning to be that he gave the two burial. "

" Right, " exclaimed Cangrande. " Florentine, I agree with you! Ezzelin was a born ruler, and, as such men usually are, somewhat harsh and violent; but nine tenths of the crimes imputed to him are inventions — forgeries of the clergy and scandal-loving people. "

" Would it were so!" sighed Dante, "at any rate where he appears upon the stage in my romance he has not yet become the monster which the chronicle, be it true or false, pictures him to be; his cruelty is only beginning to show itself in certain lines about the mouth. "

"A commanding figure," exclaimed Can-grande enthusiastically, desiring to bring him more palpably before the audience, "with black hair bristling round his great brow, as you paint him, in your Twelfth Canto, among the inhabitants of Hell. But whence have you taken this dark head?"

"It is yours," replied Dante boldly, and Cangrande felt himself flattered.

"And the rest of the characters in my story," he said with smiling menace, "I will also take from among you, if you will allow me," and he turned toward his list-eners, "I borrow your names only, leaving untouched what is innermost; for that I cannot read.

"My outward self I lend you gladly," re-sponded the Princess, whose indifference was beginning to yield.

A murmur of intense excitement now ran through the courtly circle, and "Thy story, Dante, thy story!" was heard on all sides.

"Here it is," he said, and began:—

"Where in a slender bow the course of the Brenta nears the city of Padua without touching it, there once glided over its swift but quiet waters, to the soft sound of flutes, a barque adorned with wreaths, and over-laden with a gay band in festal array. It was bearing homeward, on a lovely summer afternoon, the bride of Umberto Vicedomini. The Paduan had sought his betrothed in a cloister situated on the upper course of the river, to which, according to an old city custom, maidens of rank retired before their nuptials for pious exercises. The lady was sitting on a purple cushion in the middle of the barque between her bridegroom and his three beautiful boys. Umberto Vicedomini had lost the wife of his youth five years before when the pest raged in Padua, and, although, still in the vigor of manhood, had but reluctantly consented to a second union to gratify his sick and aged father, who daily urged it upon him.

With suspended oars the barque quietly floated onward at the will of the stream, the boatmen in an undertone accompanying the soft music with song. Suddenly there came a pause. All eyes were directed to the right bank of the river where a tall rider was

reining in his steed ; with a majestic wave
of the hand, he saluted the company in the
boat. A thrill of dismay passed from one to
the other up and down the rows of seats, the
oarsmen snatched the red caps from their
heads, and the entire party including Diana,
her bridegroom, and the boys, rose to do
reverence to Ezzelin, the ruler. With uplifted arms quickly throwing themselves into
all possible attitudes of humility and sub-
servience they turned toward the strand with
such violence that the boat lost its balance,
swayed for an instant to the right and capsized
A shriek of terror, a whirlpool, then a void in
the middle of the stream filled from time to
time with heads suddenly emerging only to
sink again, or with the floating wreaths which
had adorned the unlucky barque. Help was
not far distant. A little lower down on the
river was a small fishing-port where horses
and litters had been waiting to convey the now
drowning party to their homes in Padua.

The two first boats which started to their
relief approached rapidly from opposite directions. In the one, beside an old dwarf
with shaggy beard, stood Ezzelin the tyrant

of Padua, and the innocent cause of this catastrophe.   In the other, and coming from the
left shore, a young monk, with a boatman,
who, at the moment of the accident was
about to row the dusty pilgrim across the
stream.   Between them on the top of the
water was now seen a mass of blonde hair,
which the monk, kneeling, seized with out-
stretched arm, while the boatman held the
boat steady with all his strength on the other
side.   By means of a thick braid the monk
at last raised a head with eyes shut fast,
and assisted by Ezzelin, who was at his side,
dragged a woman, in heavily dripping garments, out of the current.   The tyrant had
sprung from his own boat into the other, and
now contemplated the lifeless face before him,
which seemed to wear an expression of both
defiance and unhappiness.   Ezzelin's gaze
betrayed a species of satisfaction — perhaps
at the repose of death, or perhaps at the
grand features before him.

"Do you know her, Astorre?" he asked of
the monk, and when the latter shook his head,
Ezzelin continued, "See! it is the wife
of your brother."

The monk cast a shy pitiful look on the still face under which the heavy eyes slowly began to open.

"Take her to the shore," commanded Ezzelin, but the monk gave her in charge to his boatman, saying, "I must seek for my brother until I find him. I will help thee, monk, said the tyrant,' yet I doubt if it is possible to save him; I saw him as he clasped his arms tightly around his boys and with the three clinging to him sank heavily into the depths below."

Meanwhile the Brenta had become covered with boats of every description. The men were fishing with hooks, poles, angles and nets, while towering over all the workers, or bending over the burdens raised, was the tall form of the governor.

"Come, Monk," he said finally, "there is nothing more here for thee to do. Umberto and his boys have now lain too long in the depths to be brought back again to life. The current has borne him far away; it will lay them all on the shore when it is tired of them."

"But do you see the tents there — yonder?

They were pitched on the strand for the reception of the wedding guests, but are now filled with their lifeless, or apparently lifeless bodies, surrounded by mourning relatives and servants. Go, Monk, and fulfil thy office. Comfort the living; bury the dead."

As he spoke the monk was already moving along the shore, and soon disappeared from sight. Diana — bride and widow of his brother in the midst of a crowd of friends, now came up to him — disconsolate indeed, but restored to her senses. The heavy hair still dripped, but upon quite a different garment, for a compassionate peasant woman in the tent had taken possession of the wedding robe and given in exchange her own dress. "Pious brother," said she to Astorre, "I am left behind; the litter intended for me in the confusion has been taken away to bear another to the city, either of the dead or the living. I pray you go with me to the house of my father-in-law, who is also thy father."

The young widow deceived herself. 'Twas not the panic and confusion which had led the servants of the elder Vicedomini to abandon her, but sheer cowardice and superstition.

They feared to take the widow to the passionate old man, and with her the tidings of the extinction of his house.

The monk, seeing many of his brotherhood engaged in acts of mercy, both within and without the tents, acceded to her request. "Yes, we will go," he said, and they turned into a road leading to the city, whose domes and slender bell towers soared into the azure heavens before their gaze. The way was crowded with hundreds of people hurrying to and from the strand. The two walked on silently in the middle of the road, often separated, but always finding each other again, and had reached the workmen's quarter. There the people were standing everywhere either talking in a loud tone, or whispering in groups — for the accident had brought the whole population to their feet. With sympathetic curiosity they gazed at the pair accidentally brought together — the one having lost a brother, the other a bridegroom.

The Monk and Diana were familiarly known to every child in Padua, — Astorre, if he did not pass for a Saint, was yet reputed

a model monk; he might have been called
" *The* monk of Padua," as being the one most
honored and revered by its inhabitants and
with reason, for he had bravely, yes, joyfully,
resigned the privileges of his high rank, and
the boundless possessions of his family, and
exposed his life without stint, in times of the
plague or other public dangers. Moreover,
with his chestnut-brown curly hair, soft,
beaming eyes and aristocratic bearing, he
was an attractive man — such as people love
to picture their saints.

Diana was, in her way, not less talked
about. Her well-developed, powerful physi-
que excited far greater admiration than more
delicate charms ever do amongst the people.
Her mother had been a German, a Hohen-
stauffen, as some asserted, though, to be sure,
only by blood, not legitimately. Germany
and Italy, like good sisters, shared the credit
of this grand figure.

However curt and reserved Diana might
have appeared to her equals she was always
accessible to those beneath her. She en-
couraged the poor people to consult her
about their business matters, gave them clear

and concise information, and kissed the rag-
gedest of the children. She spent and gave
away money without scruple or hesitation,
perhaps, because her father, the old Pizziguerra, the richest Paduan, after Vicedomini,
was at the same time the most vulgar miser,
and Diana was ashamed of her father's vice.

The loving people in their hours of gossip
at taverns and elsewhere, married her every
month to some one of the distinguished
Paduans, but the reality did not respond to
these pious wishes. Three obstacles impeded
a marriage settlement: Diana's high-arched
and often frowning brows — her father's
hard closed fists, and the blind attachment
of her brother Germano to the tyrant
whose possible destruction would involve
the faithful servant, and all his family. At
last Umberto Vicedomini was betrothed to
her, without love, as the gossips said; — and
now he lay in the Brenta!

Meanwhile the two were so absorbed in
their natural grief that they neither heard
nor heeded the eager talk which went on at
their heels. Not that the bare fact of the
monk and the lady walking together gave

any occasion for remark. It seemed quite in
order since it was the monk's duty to comfort her, and since they must both go the
same way; for were they not the most appro-
priate messengers to bear the sad tidings to
the old Vicedomini?

The women had lamented that Diana
should be forced to marry a man who accepted her merely as a kind of substitute
for his dear departed wife, and pitied her in
the same breath for having lost this man before the marriage.

The men, on the other hand, discussed
with gesticulations and violence the burning
question which the drowning in the Brenta
of the four heirs of the first Paduan family
had opened. The wealth of the Vicedomini
was proverbial — the head of the family, as
shrewd as he was able and energetic, had
succeeded in remaining on good footing with
the tyrant, four times excommunicated, and
the church, which had put him under the ban,
—had refused all his life to busy himself even
in the slightest degree with political matters,
but had devoted a tenacious and magnificent
strength of will to the one aim of increasing

the prosperity and worldly possessions of his
family. Now this was annihilated. His
eldest son and his grandchildren lay in the
Brenta. His second and third sons had in
this same unlucky year, only a few months
before, vanished from the earth. The tyrant
had claimed the first and left him behind
on one of his wild battlefields. The other,
of whom the unprejudiced father had made
a merchant in Venetian style, had been cru-
cified by pirates on a coast in the Orient,
his ransom having arrived too late. His
fourth was Astorre — the monk. That with
his dying breath the father would attempt
to free Astorre from his monastic vows,
the quick-witted Paduans did not for a moment question. Whether he would succeed
and the monk consent was now matter of
dispute in the excited little streets.

Finally the strife became so noisy and
fierce that even the grief-absorbed monk
could no longer remain in doubt as to who
was meant by the "egli" and "ella" which
were heard on all sides. For this reason, and
more for his companion's sake than for his
own, he turned into a grass-grown path his

sandals knew full well, for it led along the damp decaying walls which surrounded his cloister. Here it was cool enough to make them shiver, but the dreadful news had reached even this secluded spot. Through the open windows of the refectory, built into the thick wall, sounded the clatter of plates at the belated dinner; the catastrophe had disturbed times and hours all over the city. The conversation of the brothers at the table was so unusually loud and disputatious — so full of "inibus" and "atibus" (the monks spoke in Latin), that he knew they were discussing the same problem with the people in the streets. And though perhaps he did not quite take in the substance of their talk, still he could not help knowing of whom they talked. But what he did discover was —— "

In the midst of his sentence Dante gave a sidelong glance at the aristocratic young priest who had concealed himself behind his neighbor.

" Two burning hollow eyes, peering at him and the woman who walked by his side. They belonged to an unfortunate creature, a wretched monk, named Serapion, who was consuming himself body and soul in the cloister. With his fevered imagination he had instantly conceived that the Brother Astorre would now no longer be obliged to toil and fast, denying himself according to the rule of St. Francis; but that by the humor of Death he was restored to all his worldly joys and possessions — and he envied him madly. He had been waiting for his return home that he might study his own face and read in it what the monk had resolved upon. His eyes devoured the woman and followed her steps:

Astorre with his sister-in-law finally turned into a square surrounded by four city-castles, where they entered a low door leading to the most distinguished among them. Upon a stone seat in the courtyard two persons were resting, one a fresh young German clad in armor from head to foot, the other a grey-headed Saracen. The German who was stretched out asleep had laid his blond curly head in the lap of the unbeliever, who likewise slumbering, nodded his snow-white beard in fatherly fashion over him.

The two belonged to Ezzelin's body guard, which in imitation of his father-in-law, the Emperor Frederick, was composed of an equal number of Germans and Saracens. The tyrant was in the palace. He had thought it his duty to visit the old Vice-domini. In fact Astorre and Diana now heard upon the winding stairs the few quiet words in which Ezzelin was attempting to argue with the old man, who wholly beside himself, was weeping and cursing in a loud voice. They remained standing at the entrance to the hall among the crowd of pale menials who were trembling in every limb. The old man had heaped upon them the most violent oaths, and doubling up his fist chased them all out of his room because they had brought the unlucky tidings so tardily and then hardly dared to stammer them out. Added to this they had heard the step of the terrible tyrant in the house. It was forbidden to announce Ezzelin's approach anywhere on pain of death — unhindered like a spirit he entered houses and chambers.

"And you inform me of this so coolly,

cruel man," stormed out the Vicedomini in
his despair, "as you would tell the loss of a
horse, or a harvest! You have murdered
the four — who but you? What was the
need of your riding to the strand precisely at
that hour? Why should you greet them
upon the Brenta? You did it to injure me.
Do you hear?"

"Fate," replied Ezzelin."

"Fate!" yelled the old man, "fate—star-
gazing — conjurations and conspiracies —
heads cut off—women flung from the pavement below—young men dropping from their
horses, in your crazy fool-hardy battles,
pierced through with a hundred arrows:—
this is your age and rule, Ezzelin, you cursed
damned one! You drag us all along your
bloody path; all life, and even death itself,
near you, is violent and unnatural. Nobody
meets his end any longer as a repentant
Christian in his bed."

"You do me wrong," said the tyrant, "I
have nothing to do with the church, it is
true;—'tis a matter of indifference to me —
but I have never prevented you and yours
from alliance with it; this you know, or

you would not dare to exchange letters
with the Holy See. Why are you twisting
that paper in your hands to conceal from
me the Papal seal? An indulgence? — a
letter? Give it to me! verily a letter. May
I read it? Do you allow me?"

"'Thy patron the Holy Father writes to
thee that should thy lineage become extinct
up to the fourth and last, the monk — he,
ipso facto, would be released from his vow
if with free will and of his own free choice
be returned to the world.' Cunning foe!
How many ounces of gold has this parchment cost you?"

"Dost thou dare to scoff at me?" howled
the Vicedomini. "What remains to me but
the monk, after the deaths of my second and
third son? For whom have I amassed and
hoarded up? For the worms? for thee?
Would'st thou rob me? No? Then help
me, good father." (Ezzelin, not then excommunicated, had stood godfather to the third
Vicedomini boy — the same who later sacrificed himself for him upon the battlefield);
"help me to persuade the monk to return
to the world and take a wife — command

him to do it, thou all powerful! Give him
to me in place of the son whom thou hast
slain; do this for me, if you love me."

"This is no concern of mine," answered
the tyrant, without the slightest emotion.
"If he is a true monk, as I believe he is, why
should he change his profession? That
the blood of the Vicedomini may not be
exhausted? Is the life of the world then
dependent on it? Are the Vicedomini a ne-
cessity?" At this the old man grew frantic
with rage. "Thou wicked, cruel one — murderer of my children, I see through it. Thou
— thou would'st be my heir and carry on thy
mad campaigns with my money!" Just then
he caught sight of his daughter-in-law, who
had pressed through the crowd of servants
in advance of the monk and was standing on
the threshold. Spite of his physical weakness he rushed towards her staggering;
seized and wrenched her hands apart, as if
to make her responsible for the misfortune
which had befallen them. "Where is my
son, Diana?" he gasped out. "He lies in
the Brenta," she answered sadly, and her
blue eyes grew dim.

" Where are my three grandchildren ? "

" In the Brenta," she repeated. "And you bring me yourself as a gift — you are presented to me ? " And the old man laughed discordantly-

"Would that the Almighty," she said slowly, "had drawn me deeper under the waves, and that thy children stood here in my stead ! " She was silent ; then bursting into sudden anger, " Does my presence insult you, and am I a burden to you ? " Impute the blame to him (pointing to the monk). He drew me from the water when I was already dead and restored me to life."

The old man now for the first time perceived his son, and collecting himself quickly, exhibited the powerful will which his bitter grief seemed to have steeled rather than lamed.

" Really — he drew you out of the Brenta ? H'm ! Strange. The ways of God are marvellous ! "

He grasped the monk by the shoulder and arm at once, as if to take possession of him body and soul, and dragged him along to

his great chair, into which the old man fell
without relaxing his pressure on the arm of
his unresisting son. Diana followed, knelt
down on the other side of the chair, and
leaned her head upon the arm of it, so that
only the coil of her blond hair was visible —
like some inanimate object. Opposite the
group sat Ezzelin, his right hand upon the
rolled-up letter, like a commander-in-chief
resting upon his staff.

" My son — my own one," whimpered the
dying man, with a tenderness in which truth
and cunning mingled, " my last and only
consolation. Thou staff and stay of my old
age, thou wilt not crumble like dust under
my trembling fingers. Thou must understand," he went on, already in a colder and
more practical tone, " that as things are it is
not possible for thee to remain longer in the
cloister. It is also according to the canons,
my son, is it not, that a monk whose father
is sick unto death, or impoverished, should
withdraw in order to nurse the author of his
days, or to till his father's acres? But I
need thee even more pressingly ; thy brothers
and nephews are gone, and now thou must

keep the life-torch of our house burning.
Thou art a little flame I have kindled, and
I cannot suffer it to glimmer and die out in
a narrow cell. Know one thing;"—he had
read in the warm brown eyes a genuine
sympathy, and the reverent bearing of the
monk appeared to promise blind obedience.
"I am more ill than you suppose, am I not,
Issacher?" He turned to look a spare little
man in the face, who, with phial and spoon
in his hands, had stept behind the chair of
the old Vicedomini, and now bowed his white
head in affirmation:— "I travel toward the
river; but I tell thee, Astorre, if my wish is
not granted, thy father will refuse to step into
Charon's boat, and will sit cowering on the
twilight strand."

The monk stroked the feverish hand of the
old man with tenderness, but answered quietly
in two words—"My vows!"

Ezzelin unfolded the letter. "Thy vows,"
said the old man in a wheedling tone—
"loosened strings; filed-away chains. Make
a movement and they fall. The Holy Church,
to which thy obedience is due, has declared
them null and void, There it stands written,"

and his thin finger pointed to the parchment with the Pope's seal.

The monk approached the governor, took the letter from him respectfully, and read it through, closely watched the while by four eyes. Completely dazed, he took one step backward, as if he were standing on the top of a tower and all at once saw the rampart give way.

Ezzelin seized the reeling man by the arm with the curt question, " To whom did you make your vows, monk, — to yourself or to the church ? "

" To both, of course," shrieked the old man angrily ; " these are cursed subtleties. Take care, son, or he will reduce us, Vicedomini, to beggary."

Without a trace of feeling or resentment, Ezzelin laid his right hand on his beard and swore — " If Vicedomini dies, the monk here inherits his property, and should the family become extinct with him if he love me and his native city, he shall found a hospital of such size and grandeur that the hundred cities (he meant the Italian) will envy us. Now, godfather, having cleared myself from the charge of rapacity, may I put to the monk a few questions? — have I your permission?"

The fury of the old man now rose to such a pitch as to bring on a fit of convulsions, but even then he did not release the arm of the monk.

Issacher put carefully to the pale lips a spoon filled with some strong smelling essence. The sufferer turned his head away with an effort. "Leave me in peace," he groaned; "you are the governor's physician as well," and closed his eyes again.

The Jew looked at the tyrant as if to beg forgiveness for this suspicion. "Will he return to life?" asked Ezzelin. "I think so," replied the Jew, "but not for long; I fear he will not live to see the sun go down."

The tyrant took advantage of the moment to speak to the monk who was exerting himself to the utmost to restore his father.

"Answer me, Astorre," he began, while he buried the outspread fingers of his right hand, a favorite gesture, in his beard — "how much have the three vows cost you which you took some ten years ago; for I

take it you are now about thirty? The
monk bowed assent, then raised his frank
clear eyes and said without hesitation : "The
two first, poverty and obedience, nothing — I
had no desire for possessions, and it is easy
for me to obey." He paused and blushed.

The tyrant was pleased with this simple
manliness. " Did your father compel or persuade you to choose this profession ? " " No,"
he replied ;"for three or four generations, as
the family history records, the last son of our
house has been a priest or monk, perhaps
because we needed an intercessor in Heaven,
— or it may have been considered one way to
preserve our power on earth ; — whatever the
reason, it was a time-honored custom. I
knew my destiny from childhood, and it was
not repugnant to me. No restraint was exercised over me."

"And how about that third? " He meant
the third vow; Astorre understood him.

Again blushing, but this time faintly, he
replied " It was not easy for me, still I con-
quered, like other monks who have good ad-
visers, and such I had in St. Antonius," he
added reverently.

"This meritorious saint, as you know, my Lords, lived for some years in the Franciscan cloisters at Padua," explained Dante. "Why shouldn't we know," jokingly retorted one of his hearers; "haven't we all paid our respects to the relic swimming about in the cloister pond yonder? I mean the pike, which once heard a sermon of the saints, was converted, renounced animal food, kept henceforth to the strait and narrow path, and at an advanced age remained a strict vegetarian." He choked down the end of his nonsense, for Dante frowned upon him and continued.

"What did he advise you?" asked Ezzelin. "To take up my profession in a simple straightforward way, as I would any other service, for instance, military service, which also requires obedient muscles, self-denial, and the strength to endure hardships of various kinds, although a true warrior does even feel them to be such; to till the earth in the sweat of my brow, eat moderately, fast moderately, confess neither maidens nor young women, live in the sight of God and worship His Mother not more passionately than the breviary prescribes."

The tyrant smiled, then extended his right hand toward the monk in encouragement or blessing and said, "Fortunate one, thou hast a star; with thee, to-day follows naturally upon yesterday, and will unawares usher in the morrow. Thou art something, and that not insignificant, for thou fulfillest the office of charity, which I neglect, however well I may perform a different one. If you should enter the world, which has its own laws, though it is too late for you to learn them, your clear star would become a mere fire-rocket, which after a few foolish leaps, would explode, hissing into darkness, scoffed at by the heavenly powers. One thing more, and this I say, being what I am, the Lord of Padua. Thy character has elevated my people and set them an example of self-denial. The poorest was comforted by remembering he had seen thee sharing his scanty food and doing the same hard daily work. If you throw aside the cowl as an aristocrat, wed a proud lady, and draw with full hands from the wealth of your house, you will commit a robbery on the people, who had taken possession of you as one of their own; you will create discontent

and dissatisfaction, and it would not surprise
me if a train of evils should follow in their
wake.   These things are linked together!"

"Padua, and its ruler, cannot dispense
with thee, the eyes of the multitude are
drawn to thee, and thou hast more, or certainly a nobler, spirit than thy low-born
brethren. If the people, in mad frenzy,
should threaten to murder this man," and
he pointed to Issacher, " for instance, as they
did in the time of the last plague, because he
brought them relief, who would defend him
against their insane fury until I could arrive,
and command them to halt?"

"Issacher, help me to convince the monk,"
and Ezzelin turned to the physician with a
cruel smile, "you see that even for your sake
he must not be allowed to lay aside his cowl."

"Prince," whispered the Jew, "under thy
sceptre this irrational scene, for which you
so properly exacted a bloody penalty, will
scarcely be repeated, and therefore on my
account whose faith extols, as God's greatest
blessing, the perpetuity of race, this illustrious Lord (he already substituted this title
for that of Reverend) is no longer to remain
unmarried."

Ezzelin smiled at the subtlety of the Jew.
" And whither do your own thoughts tend,
Monk?" he inquired. " They are unchanged
and persistent, yet, God forgive me, I would
that my father never woke again, that I
should be forced to oppose him cruelly. If
he had but received extreme unction!" He
kissed passionately the cheek of the fainting
man, who thereupon returned to consciousness.

Heaving a deep sigh, he raised his weary
eyelids, and from under · the gray bushy
brows directed toward the monk a supplicating look. "How is it?" he asked, "to what
hast thou doomed me, dearest — to heaven or
to hell?"

"Father," prayed Astorre in a tremulous
voice," thy time has come, only a short hour
remains, banish all earthly cares and inter-
ests, think of thy soul." "See, thy priests"
(he meant those of the parish church), "are
gathered together waiting to perform the
last sacrament."

It was so! The door of the adjacent room
had softly opened in which the faint glimmer
of lighted candles was perceptible, whilst a

choir was intoning a prelude, and the gentle vibration of a bell became audible.

Now the old man, who already felt his knees sinking into Lethe's flood, clung to the monk, as once St. Peter to the Saviour on the Sea of Gennesareth. "Thou wilt do it for my sake?" he stammered.

"If I could; if I dared," sighed the monk. "By all that is holy, my father, think on eternity, leave the earthly. Thine hour is come!"

This veiled refusal kindled the last spark of life in the old man to a blaze. "Disobedient, ungrateful one," he cried.

Astorre beckoned to the priests. "By all the devils, spare me your kneadings and salvings," raved the dying man, "I have nothing to gain, I am already like one of the damned, and must remain so in the midst of paradise, if my son wantonly repudiates me, and destroys my germ of life."

The horror-struck monk, thrilled to the soul by this frightful blasphemy, pictured his father doomed to eternal perdition. (This was his thought and he was as firmly convinced of the truth of it as I should have been in his place). He fell down on his knees before the old man, and in utter despair, bursting into tears, said: "Father, I beseech thee, have pity on thyself, and on me!"

"Let the crafty one go his way," whispered the tyrant.

The monk did not hear him. Again he gave the astounded priests a sign and the litany for the dying was about to begin.

At this the old man doubled himself up like a refractory child, and shook his head.

"Let the sly fox go where he must," admonished Ezzelin in a louder tone.

"Father, Father," sobbed the monk, his whole soul dissolved in pity.

"Illustrious Signor and Christian Brother," said the priest with unsteady voice, "are you in the frame of mind to meet your Creator and Saviour?" The old man took no notice.

"Are you firm as a believer in the Holy Trinity?" answer me, Signor," said the priest, and then turned pale as a sheet, for "Cursed and denied be it for ever and ever," fell from the dying man's lips. "Cursed and —"

"No more," cried the monk springing to his feet. "Father, I resign myself to thy will. Do with me what you choose if only you will not throw yourself into the flames of Hell."

The old man gasped as after some terrible exertion; then gazed about him with an air of relief, I had almost said of pleasure. Groping, he seized the blonde hair of Diana, lifted her up from her knees, took her right hand, which she did not refuse, opened the cramped hand of the monk and laid the two together: —

"Binding, in presence of the most Holy Sacrament!" he exclaimed triumphantly, and blessed the pair. The monk did not gainsay it, while Diana closed her eyes.

"Now quick, Reverend Fathers, there is need of haste I think, and I am now in a Christian frame of mind."

The monk and his affianced bride would fain have stepped behind the train of priests. "Stay," muttered the dying man, "stay where my comforted eyes may look upon you until they close in death." Astorre and Diana were thus with clasped hands obliged to wait and watch the expiring glance of the obstinate old man.

The latter murmured a short confession, received the last sacrament and breathed his final breath, as they were anointing his feet, while the priests uttered in his already deaf ears those sublime words, " Rise, Christian Soul." The dead face bore the unmistakeable expression of triumphant cunning.

The tyrant sat, whilst all around were upon their knees, and with calm attention observed the performance of the sacred office, much like a savant studying on a sarcophagus the representation of some religious rites of an ancient people. He now approached the dead man and closed his eyes.

He then turned to Diana. " Noble Lady," said he, " let us go home, your parents, even if assured of your safety, will long to see you."

" Prince, I thank you, and will follow," she answered, but she did not withdraw her hand from that of the monk, whose eyes until then she had avoided. Now she looked her betrothed full in the face, and said in a deep, but melodious voice, whilst her cheeks glowed: " My Lord and Master, we

could not let your father's soul perish ; thus
have I become yours. Hold your faith to
me, better than to the cloister. Your brother
did not love me ; forgive me for saying it,
I speak the simple truth. You will have
in me a good and obedient wife, but I have
two peculiarities, which you must treat with
indulgence. I am hot with anger if any
attack is made on my honor or my rights,
and I am most exacting in regard to the
fulfilment of a promise once made Even
as a child I was so. I have few wishes, and
desire nothing unreasonable, but when a
thing has once been shown and promised me,
I insist upon possessing it, and I lose my
faith, and resent injustice more than other
women, if the promise I have received is not
faithfully kept. But how can I allow myself
to talk in this way to you, my Lord, whom I
scarcely know? I have done. Farewell, my
husband, grant me nine days to mourn your
brother." At this she slowly released her
hand from his and disappeared with the
tyrant.

Meanwhile, the band of priests had borne
away the corpse to place it upon a bier in
the palace chapel, and to bless it.

Astorre was once more alone, in his for-
feited monk's dress, which now covered a
breast filled with repentance. A host of
servants who had listened, and sufficiently
comprehended the strange proceeding, approached their new master shyly, and in
submissive attitudes, being perplexed and
intimidated, less by the change of masters
than by the supposed sacrilege of the broken
vow, for the reading of the papal letter had
not reached their ears.   But how could Astorre force himself to grieve for the loss of
his father?   He had recovered the strength
of his own will, and the suspicion had stolen
into his mind, nay, the maddening certainty
had overwhelmed him that the dying man
had taken unfair advantage of his pity and
deceived his simple faith.   He discovered in
the despair of the old man the last resource
of cunning, and in his mad blasphemies, a
crafty purpose on the threshold of death.
He next turned his thoughts, with unwil-
lingness, even aversion, to the wife who had
fallen to him.   The idea of loving her, not
from his own heart, but as his dead brother's
proxy, chimed in with his perverted monkish

reasoning, although his healthy honest nature revolted against such a niggardly ex-
pedient.   Now that he considered her his
own, he could not repress a certain amazement at his wife's having addressed him in
such concise terms, and at the frank, uncom-
promising honesty with which she adjusted
her claims.   Truly a sturdier and more substantial being than the ideal woman of the
legend!   He had imagined women gentler.

Suddenly Astorre was reminded of the
contradiction between his monastic dress
and all these feelings and reflections.   He
was ashamed of his cowl, and it grew irksome
to him.   "Bring me worldly garments," he
ordered, and the officious servants hastened
to obey his wish.   He was soon dressed in a
suit which had been his brother's; they having
been about the same height.

At this moment his father's fool, named
Gocciola, threw himself at his feet, and
would do him homage, not, however, like the
others, to ask the continuance of his service,
but to pray for dismissal and permission to
change his profession; he said he was weary
of the world, and it would ill become his gray

hair to go into the next life in cap and bells.
Thus wailing and whining, he took possession of the monk's cast-off garments, which
the servants had not dared to touch. Then
his inconstant brain turned a complete somer-
sault, and he said greedily, " I think I'll wait
and eat Amarella once more before I bid
farewell to the world and its delusions. We
shall not have to wait long here, I think, for
a wedding." And he licked the corners of
his mouth with his flabby tongue. Then
bending one knee before the Monk, he shook
his bells and sprang away, dragging rope and
cowl behind him.

Amarella, or Amare, Dante explained, was
the name given by the Paduans to their
wedding-cake, on account of its flavor of
bitter almonds, and also in graceful allusion
to the verb of the first conjugation. Here
he paused, and, shading brow and eyes with
his hand, was evidently considering how to
go on with the romance.

During the interim, the Majordomo of the
Prince, an Alsatian named Burcardo, with
measured steps, ceremonious bows, and pro-
fuse apologies for thus disturbing the enter-

tainment, presented himself before Cangrande to ask for commands about some do-
mestic matters. The Germans were in that
day no rare apparition at the Ghibelline
courts of Italy ; indeed they were sought and
preferred to the natives, because of their
honesty and quickness in apprehending ceremonies and customs.

When Dante, raised his head again, he
saw the Alsatian, and heard the dire havoc
he was making among the Italian consonants,
which, while it amused the courtiers, offended
the sensitive ear of the poet. His eyes
lingered with evident pleasure on the two
young men, Ascanio and the mail-clad knight,
and at last, thoughtfully on the ladies, the
princess Diana, whose marble cheeks were
now suffused with a faint flush of animation,
and Antiope, the friend of Cangrande, a
pretty sprightly creature. He then continued : —

" Behind the city-castle of the Vicedomini
there formerly spread (though to-day the illustrious race has so long been extinct, that
the plot of ground has wholly changed its
character) a district of such extent as to fur-

nish pasturage for cattle, preserves for stag
and deer, ponds full of fish, deep shady woods
and sunny vineyards. On a brilliant morning, seven days after the funeral, the monk,
Astorre, was sitting in the dark shade of a
cedar, with his back against the trunk, and
the points of his shoes stretching out into
the burning sunlight. (This title of "Monk"
he retained among the Romans to the end
of his short pilgrimage upon earth.) He
was lying, rather than sitting, opposite a
fountain, where, from the mouth of a great
stone face, gushed a cool flood. As he was
dreaming or thinking, I know not which,
two young men, one in armor, the other in
a handsome travelling costume, sprang from
their dust-covered steeds, and with rapid
steps crossed the hot, sunny square in front
of the palace. Ascanio and Germano, such
were the rider's names, were favorites of the
Governor, and had been youthful companions
of the monk, with whom, in brotherly fashion,
they had studied and played up to his fif-
teenth year, or the beginning of his novitiate.
Ezzelin had sent them with despatches to his
brother-in-law, Emperor Frederick. The two

were on their way back to the tyrant bearing
replies to important questions, and added to
these, the news of the day, and a copy, made
in the Imperial Chancery, of a pastoral letter
addressed to the Christian Clergy, wherein
the Holy Father accused the great-minded
Emperor, in the face of the world, of the
most utter godlessness.   Although entrusted
with this portentous document, as well as
other weighty missives, the two could not
find it in their hearts to rush past the home
of their old play-fellow, which was directly
en route to the tyrant's castle, without stopping to offer him a word of sympathy.   At
the last inn before reaching Padua, where,
without leaving the stirrup, they had let the
horses drink, they had heard from the gossiping landlord of the great city disaster and
the still greater city scandal, of the loss of
the wedding-barque, and the discarded cowl
of the monk with all the attendant circumstances, except that of uniting the hands of
Diana and Astorre, which had not yet been
made public.   Indissoluble are the bonds
which chain us to the companions of our
childhood.   Startled by the strange fate of

Astorre, the two could not rest until they had beheld, with their own eyes, a friend thus restored to the world and to them. During many years they had seen the monk only by chance in the street, where they greeted him with a kindly but somewhat distant bow made the deeper by a sincere reverence.

Gocciola, whom they found in the court of the palace munching a biscuit, as he sat swinging his legs over a bit of wall, led them into the garden. As they strolled along, the fool entertained the gentlemen not with the tragic fate of the house, but with his own affairs, which seemed to him of more importance. He said that he was fervently striving for a blessed end, and swallowed the rest of the biscuit without chewing it with his loose teeth, so that it all but choked him. The grotesque faces he made up, together with his maudlin talk about living in a cell, caused Ascanio.to break into such merry peals of laughter as would have driven every cloud out of the sky if the day had not revelled for its own delight in all the glowing colors.

Ascanio did not hesitate to banter the

" Little Drop " in order the sooner to be rid
of this annoying mortal. " Poor fellow," he
began, " you will not gain the cell, for, between ourselves, the tyrant has cast longing
eyes on you. Let me tell you; he has four
fools, the Stoic, the Epicurean, the Platonic
and the Skeptic, as he calls them. These
four, when the grave tyrant desires to unbend,
place themselves, at a sign from him, in the
four corners of a hall, on whose vaulted
ceiling the planets and heavenly constella-
tions are pictured. My Uncle in everyday
dress steps into the middle of the room, claps
his hands, and the philosophers with a skip
exchange corners. Day before yesterday,
the Stoic died weeping and moaning, for
the insatiable creature had devoured many
pounds of vermicelli. My Uncle hinted to
me, cursorily, that he thinks of replacing him
and will entreat the Monk, your new master,
to grant him you, as a contribution from his
inheritance, Oh, Gocciola! so the matter
stands. Ezzelin is going to try to capture
you! Who knows whether he may not be
right upon your heels at this moment?
This was in allusion to the ubiquity of the

tyrant which kept the Paduans in a constant state of alarm. Gocciola uttered a shriek, as if the hand of the mighty one had fallen upon his shoulder, looked around trembling, and though there was nothing behind him but his own little shadow, with chattering teeth fled away to some hiding place.

" I erase the fools of Ezzelin," said Dante, with a gesture of his hand, as if he held a pen and were writing a romance, instead of telling it. " This feature is untrue, Ascanio lied. It is nowise conceivable that a nature so serious and grand as Ezzelin's could have found pleasure in feeding fools, or listening to their silly chatter." This was a hit the Florentine directed at his host, on whose mantle Gocciola sat leering and grinning at the poet.

Cangrande did not appear to heed it, but secretly promised himself to pay Dante back, with interest, at the first opportunity.

Satisfied, and almost gaily, Dante continued his narration.

"Soon the friends discovered the uncowled monk leaning against the trunk of a pine."

"A cedar, Dante," corrected the Princess,
who had listened with increasing attention.
"A cedar, sunning the tips of his feet. He
did not observe his guests coming up on
either side, so deeply was he absorbed in
his empty — or was it over-burdened? —
thoughts. Ascanio stooped, picked a blade
of grass and tickled the monk's nose until
he sneezed three times lustily. Astorre
warmly grasped the hands of his youthful
playfellows, and drew them left and right
down upon the grass beside him. "Now
what do you say to it all?" he asked in a
tone rather timid than defiant. "Well, first
my hearty praise of your prior and your
cloister" laughed Ascanio, "for keeping you
so fresh; you look younger than either of us.
To be sure, the trig-fitting dress and smooth
chin may have some share in this rejuvena-
tion. Do you know that you are a handsome
man? Here, dropt under this huge cedar
you are like the first man, by God created
thirty years of age, as the learned assert,
and I," he went on with an artless expression,
as he saw the monk blush at his audacity, "I
am truly the last to blame you that you have

freed yourself from the monk's hood, for to preserve his race is the instinct of every living thing."

"It was not my wish, nor my voluntary decision," the monk acknowledged truthfully. "Reluctantly I yielded to the will of my dying father."

"Really!" Ascanio said, and smiled. "Do not tell this, Astorre, to anybody but to us who love you; to others this lack of independence would seem ridiculous. I pray you take care, Astorre, that in developing the man out of the monk you do not overstep the boundaries of good taste. The difficult transition should be made by delicate gradations. Accept counsel; travel a year, perhaps, visit the Court of the Emperor; messengers are constantly running from thence to Padua and back. Allow yourself to be sent by Ezzelin to Palermo. You will there become acquainted with the most perfect Knight, and a man wholly free from prejudice. I mean our Frederick the Second; and you will there also be brought to understand women, and wean yourself from the monkish habit of either disparaging them too much, or idolizing them. The character of the ruler colors court and city. Life here in Padua under my uncle, the tyrant, has grown wild, extravagant, arbitrary, and gives you a false picture of the world. Palermo, when under the most humane of all rulers, play and earnest, duty and pleasure, loyalty and fickleness, good faith and prudent mistrust, mingle in just proportions, affords a vastly truer picture. There, trifle away a twelve-month, or share in a campaign, without exposing yourself rashly. Keep your destination ever in view, but just remind yourself of the way to manage horse and sabre; as a boy you knew how to do it well. Keep your gay brown eyes, which, by the torch of Aurora, sparkle and glow since you left the cloister, open on all sides, and return to us a man able to command himself and others."

"He must marry a Swabian yonder at the Emperor's court," added the mail-clad friend good-naturedly. "They are more trustworthy and honest than our women." "Will you be silent?" admonished Ascanio, "save me from your heavy flaxen braids." But the monk pressed Germano's right hand which he had not let go.

"Frankly, Germano, what do you say to all this?" "To what," said Germano brusquely. "Why, to my new position?"

"Astorre my friend," answered the moustached youth, somewhat embarrassed, "when a thing is done, one no longer asks for advice, but simply defends the act; if you must have my opinion, however, see here, Astorre, violated faith, broken vows, desertion of one's colors etc., to these things in Germany we give harsh names. Of course, with you it was something quite different, not to be compared — then your dying father! Astorre, my friend, you have acted well, only the contrary would have been better still. This is my opinion," he concluded cordially.

"Then if you had been here, you would have refused me the hand of your sister, Germano?"

Germano looked as if a thunderbolt had fallen at his feet. "The hand of my sister Diana, who is now in mourning for your brother?" "The same — she is my betrothed." "Ah! glorious," cried the worldly-wise Ascanio, and "Delightful," responded

Germano, "let me embrace thee brother,
brother-in-law," for the soldier, in spite of his
abruptness, had good manners. But he
suppressed a sigh. Heartily as he esteemed
his austere sister, he would have selected a
wholly different woman for the monk sitting
beside him.

So he twisted his moustache, and Ascanio
hastened to give the conversation a different
turn. "Astorre," said he, pleasantly, "we
must begin to get acquainted with each
other anew; no less than fifteen contempla-
tive years in a cloister lie between our
childhood and to-day. Not that, in the
meantime, we have changed our natures, for
who does that? but we have developed; Germano, for instance, has gained fame and
glory on the battle-field as a warrior, yet we
have to accuse him of having become half-
German. He," and Ascanio doubled up his
arm as if pouring the contents of a whole
beaker down his throat, "afterward grows
melancholy, or quarrelsome. Then he de-
spises our sweet Italian and says boastfully
'I shall speak German with you,' and growls
out the bearish sounds of a savage tongue.

His servants turn pale, his creditors fly, and
our Paduan women turn their stately backs
upon him. This is perhaps why he has
remained a maiden knight like yourself
Astorre," and he laid his hand confidingly
on the monk's shoulder.

Germano laughed heartily and answered,
pointing to Ascanio. "And he has found
his vocation, which is to be the perfect
courtier. "

"Here you are mistaken, Germano," replied Ezzelin's favorite, "my aim has only
been to enjoy life, to be easy and gay." As
proof of this, he hailed the child of the gar-
dener, who was stealing by in the distance,
looking askance at her new master, the monk,
and bade her come nearer. The pretty
little thing bore on her laughing head a
basket heaped up with figs and grapes, and
looked much more roguish than shy or
bashful. Ascanio sprang up, threw his left
arm round the maiden's slender waist, and
with his right pulled a bunch of grapes out
of her basket, trying at the same time to
kiss her full rosy lips. The coy maiden
blushed, but kept quite still for fear of spill-

ing her fruit. The monk, however, turned
from the gay courtier with displeasure, and
the little girl, frightened at his gesture, ran
off as fast as she could, strewing the path
behind her flying feet with the fruit. Ascanio, holding his own bunch of grapes in
his hand, stooped and picked up two others,
one of which he offered Germano, who
flung it contemptuously into the grass. The
good-natured fellow passed the other over
to the monk, who at first allowed it to lie
untouched, but after a while thoughtlessly
tasted one grape, and soon a second and a
third.

"A courtier" continued Ascanio, as,
amused at the prudery of the thirty-years
old monk, he threw himself down again beside him on the grass, "don't you believe it
Astorre! believe exactly the contrary. I am
the only one who, quietly and in plain words,
can persuade my uncle not to become un-
merciful, and, while a ruler, to remain a man!

"He is only just and true to himself,"
added Germano.

"Oh, his justice, and the logic of his
deeds!" said Ascanio sadly. "Padua is a feoff

of the Empire; Ezzelin is governor. Whoever is dissatisfied with him rebels against the Empire; and rebels, traitors must be—" he could not bring his lips to utter it— "horrible!" he murmured. "And yet, to speak out frankly, why can't we Italians manage our own lives under this blue sky of ours? Why, forever, this misty phantom of the Empire stifling our breath? I speak not for myself; my fate is bound up with that of my uncle. If the Emperor dies— whom God preserve!—all Italy, with cursing and swearing, will overthrow the tyrant Ezzelin and will strangle the nephew along with him." Ascanio gazed at the luxurious earth, the radiant heavens, and uttered a sigh.

"Both of us," added Germano coolly, "but not yet awhile; the governor, according to prophecy, is to maintain his power firmly for a long time to come. The learned Guido Bonatti and Paul of Bagdad, who might sweep the dust from the streets with his long beard, although usually in passionate contradiction to one another, have with accord unriddled for him a new and cu-

rious constellation in the following manner.
Sooner, or later, a son of the peninsula is to
win undivided power over it, with the help
of a German Emperor, who for his part, is,
on the other side of the mountains to unite
all the Germans under the sway of one solid
Imperial Crown.   Is Frederic this Emperor?
Is this king Ezzelin?   God alone can tell.
Who knows the time and the hour? but the
governor has staked our heads and his re-
nown upon it."

"A tissue of rationalism and blind delusion," said Ascanio, annoyed, whilst the
monk heard, with amazement, of the might
of the stars, the unbridled ambition of the
ruler, and the all-engrossing rush and whirl
of worldly life.

The spectre of the cruelty of Ezzelin,
whom, in his innocence, he had looked upon
as incorporated justice, began also to alarm
him.

Ascanio responded to his doubts and fears
by ejaculating with emphasis, "That dark-
browed Guido and the bearded heathen, may
they both find a miserable end! They mis-
lead my uncle, catering to his lusts and

humors, whilst they persuade him that he is only doing what is necessary. Have you ever observed him, Germano? how at his frugal meal he only colors the water in his transparent crystal cup with three or four drops of blood-red Sicilian? how attentively his eyes follow this blood as it slowly clouds and permeates the pure stream? or how he loves to close the lids of the dead, so that it has become a courtesy to invite the governor to a death-bed, as to a feast, and to commit to him this last sad duty? Ezzelin, my Prince, do not, I pray thee become cruel!" exclaimed the youth, overcome by his feelings.

"No, I will not, my nephew," said a voice behind him. It was Ezzelin, who had approached unseen, and though no. listener, had heard the last bitter supplication.

The three young men rose quickly and greeted the ruler, who accepted a seat beside them on the bank. His face was calm as the mask at the fountain.

"You, my messengers," he said, addressing Ascanio and Germano, "how came it that you sought out this man (he nodded lightly to the monk) before me?"

"He was our playfellow and he has met with strange vicissitudes of late," said his nephew by way of excuse, and Ezzelin let it pass. He took the letters which Ascanio handed to him on bended knee and, with the exception of the Papal Bull, crowded them all into the bosom of his dress. "See here," said he, "the latest; read it aloud, Ascanio, your eyes are younger than mine."

Ascanio read the Apostolic letter, whilst Ezzelin, burying his right hand in his beard, listened with demoniac satisfaction.

The triple-crowned writer began by giving the enlightened Emperor the name of "Apocalyptic Monster." "This is nothing new," said the tyrant, "I, too, was called by all sorts of extravagant names until I admonished the Pontifex that whoever had anything to say to Ezzelin must henceforth upbraid him in classic language. What name does he give me this time? I am curious to know; hunt up the passage, Ascanio, in which he reproaches my father-in-law for his bad associate. Give it to me!" He seized the letter and soon found the place. The Pope accused the Emperor of loving the husband of his daughter, Ezzelin da Romano, the greatest criminal on the inhabited globe.

"Correct," assented Ezzelin, and gave Ascanio back the letter. "Now read to me the sins of the Emperor, nephew," he said smiling.

Ascanio read on: "Frederic has said, three imposters — Moses, Mahomet, and "— he hesitated —"had deceived the world." "Superficial!" exclaimed Ezzelin with a frown, "they had their stars, but whether he said it or not, the remark engraves itself, and outweighs for him who wears the tiara, an army and a fleet; — proceed!"

Now followed a curious anecdote. "Frederic, riding through a cornfield, had joked with his attendants, and in blasphemous allusion to the sacred bread, recited these lines : —

As many Gods there are as ears of grain,
They quickly shoot aloft through sun and rain,
And wave their golden heads on hill and plain." .

Ezzzelin thought a moment. "Curious!" he whispered. "My memory has preserved this little verse somewhere. It is absolutely

authentic. The Emperor recited it to me,
with a merry laugh, as we were riding together in sight of the temple ruins of Enna,
through those exuberant cornfields with
which the goddess Ceres has blessed Sicilian
soil. I remember it with the same clearness
that shone over the Isle on that summer day.
I am not the one, however, who repeated
this conceit to the Pontifex; I am too grave
a man to do that. Who did it? I appeal to
you. There were three of us and the third
— of this, too, I am as certain as of the
luminous sun above us (a beam fell straight
into the arbor) was Peter de Vinca, — the
inseparable companion of the Emperor.
May the pious Chancellor have feared for
his soul and relieved his conscience by a
letter to Rome? Does a Saracen ride forth
to-day? Yes? Quick, Ascanio, I will dic-
tate a few lines."

Ascanio drew out a little tablet and
pencil, and, dropping upon his right knee,
used the left as a desk. "Illustrious Prince
and beloved father-in-law, one hurried word.
The little verse in the Bull (you have far too
much mind to repeat yourself) was heard

only by four ears, mine and those of your Peter, a year ago, in the cornfields of Enna, at the time you called me to your court, and I rode with you over the island. Have the winds of heaven proved treacherous and borne these lines to the Vicar of St. Peter? If you love me and yourself, Prince, rack your Chancellor's brains for an answer."

"Bloody suggestion! I will not write it, my hand trembles," cried Ascanio, turning pale, and he threw his pencil away.

"Official duty," Germano said drily, picked up the pencil and finished the letter which he thrust under his helmet. "It will go off to-day. As regards my simple self I never liked this Capuan, he has a veiled look."

The monk Astorre shivered in spite of the mid-day sun. After his peaceful cloister life the suspicion and treachery of the world seemed to him like the slippery coils of a viper he was grasping in his hands. A stern rebuke from Ezzelin, as he rose from his stone seat banished his reverie.

"Say, monk, why do you bury yourself in your castle. You have not left it since you donned the world's garb. You shrink from

public opinion?   Face it boldly, it will yield,
but make a single attempt at flight and it
will hang upon your heels.   Have you visi-
ted Diana?   The week of mourning is past.
I advise you to invite your kinsfolk and
marry Diana to-day."

"Then be off with you to your remotest
castle," concluded Ascanio.

"I do not counsel this," said the tyrant,
"no fear, no flight.   To-day be married and
to-morrow give the wedding feast with masks.
Valete."   He departed, motioning Germano
to follow him."

"May I interrupt," asked Cangrande, who
had courteously waited until a pause came
in the narrative.

"You are Lord and Master" peevishly
replied the Florentine.

"Do you really impute to our immortal
Emperor that word 'impostor' as applied to
three great souls?"

"*Non lignet.*"

"I mean in your secret soul?"

With a motion of the head Dante nega-
tived the question.

"And yet you have condemned him as

being one of the ungodly, to the sixth circle
in your hell. How could you do this? jus-
tify yourself."

" Illustrissimo," replied the Florentine,
"the Commedia expresses the judgment and
sentence of this age, which, whether justly
or unjustly, reads the most frightful blasphemies on that sublime brow. It is not for me
to oppose the opinion of the pious, perhaps,
however, the Future will judge him quite
differently."

" My Dante," said Cangrande, a second
time, " dost thou believe Petrus de Vinca innocent of this crime against the Emperor? "

"*Non lignet.*"

" I mean in your inmost soul? "

Dante again shook his head.

"Yet you allow the traitor to affirm his
innocence in your Commedia."

" Prince, have I any right, in lack of actual
proof, to accuse one more son of this Italian
peninsula where we know of so much
double-dealing and knavery? "

" Dante, noble poet, you do not believe in
the guilt and you condemn; you do believe
in the guilt and you absolve." He then in

playful fashion attempted to go on himself
with the story.   " The monk and Ascanio left
the garden and entered the Hall."

But Dante caught the broken thread —
saying, " Not so — they mounted to a small
room in the tower; the same which Astorre
had occupied, when a curly-haired boy, for
he could not at once accustom himself to the
large and magnificent rooms, now his own,
nor had he as yet touched any portion of the
golden hoard bequeathed to him.   At a commanding gesture from Ascanio the stiff and
surly looking Major-domo Burcardo, followed
the two friends."

Cangrande's major-domo, who had returned
to the hall in order to listen to the story,
now found himself so faithfully mirrored in
it, that he deemed this misuse of his stately
person most unseemly, in fact, presumptious,
from the mouth of a stranger, to whom he had
given the simplest room imaginable in the
palace.   What the others enjoyed as a joke
he resented as an insult with frowning brows
and angry glance.

The Florentine seemed to relish his indignation and went on with his tale.

"Worthy Sir," Ascanio addressed the Major-domo (did I say he was by birth an Alsatian?) "how does one get married in Padua? Astorre and I find ourselves inexperienced in this science."

The master of ceremonies struck an attitude and gazed fixedly at his master without deigning a look at Ascanio, who according to his notion, had no right to demand anything of him.

"*Destingendum est*" said he solemnly; "there are three distinct ceremonies to be observed; the wooing, the espousals, and the wedding."

"Where does all this stand written down?" enquired Ascanio laughing.

"*Ecce!*" replied the Majordomo as he unfolded before them a big book which he always carried about with him. "Here!" and he pointed with the first finger of his left hand to the title. "The ceremonies of Padua, collected after the most careful researches for the pious use and benefit of all respectable and honorable people by Messer Godoscalco Burcardo." He turned over the leaves and read. "Section 1st. The Wooing.

Paragraph 1st. The earnest wooer brings with him a friend of like position as legal witness, and — " " By the superabundant merits of my patron saint, spare us the ante and post, the wooing and wedding. Serve up your middle course. How are Espousals conducted in Padua ? "

" In Batooa " crowed the irritated Alsatian, whose barbarous pronunciation was exaggerated by his excitement, "for patrician sposalizio the twelve noble families must be invited" —he counted them over from memory — " ten days beforehand, no earlier, no later, by the Majordomo of the Bridegroom attended by six servants. Before this assembly of nobles the rings are exchanged. The guests drink Cybrian and eat Amarella."

" Heaven preserve our teeth," laughed Ascanio, and snatching the book he read through the names of the families, six of which had been erased with broad strokes. They had probably been involved in some conspiracy against the tyrant and had thus perished.

" Now listen, old man," commanded Ascanio, acting for the monk, who had sunk into a chair, and, lost in thought, surrendered himself to his friendly guardian. " Make your rounds with the other six good-for-nothings at once, this very hour, without delay, do you understand? and give the invitations for this evening at vesper time."

" Ten days beforehand," repeated Messer Burcardo, majestically, as if proclaiming an Imperial law.

" To-day, and for to-day, obstinate fellow." " Impossible," said the Majordomo quietly, " would you change the course of the planets and the seasons ? "

" You rebel ! do you want your throat ornamented with a rope, old man?" said Ascanio with a peculiar smile.

This sufficed. Burcardo understood Ezzelin had commanded, and the stiff-necked pedant yielded without grumbling; such an iron rod did the tyrant hold over his people.

" But you are NOT to invite the two ladies Canossa; Signora Olympia, and Signorina Antiope."

" Why not these ? " and the monk suddenly sprang to his feet as if touched by a magic wand. The empty air took form and color and a picture rose before his fantasy the bare outlines of which captivated his whole soul.

"Because the Countess Olympia is a fool, Astorre. Do you not know the poor woman's history? Ah! you were at that time in swathing bands, or, to speak more properly, in the cowl. It was three years ago when the leaves were sere and yellow."

"No, 'twas in the summer, Ascanio" said the monk, "the anniversary must be fast approaching."

"You are right! Do you then know the story? But how should you? Count Canossa was suspected of having secret dealings with the legate, was watched, seized and condemned. The Countess threw herself at the feet of my uncle, but he wrapped himself in unapproachable silence; she then allowed herself to be basely deceived by one of the chamberlains who, for the sake of the money he could make out of her, promised that the Count should receive his pardon before the block. This was not fulfilled, and when they brought to her the Count, beheaded, maddened by the sudden change from hope to despair, she flung herself out of the window, but marvellous to relate, apparently suffered no injury except the spraining of her foot. From that day to this, however, her mind has been deranged. If our natural moods imperceptibly resolve themselves one into another, as the light of day gradually fades and is lost in the darkness of night, hers, on the contrary, pass abruptly from bright to dark, twelve times in twelve hours. A prey to the bitterest unrest this miserable woman hurries from her deserted city-palace to her country house, and from there back again to the city in a state of constant bewilderment. To-day she threatens to marry her daughter to the son of a farmer, because only in the humbler walks of life security and peace is to be found ; to-morrow the most aristocratic lover, (who, to be sure, through fear of such a mother is not likely to present himself,) is considered scarcely grand enough."

If Ascanio, in the midst of his talk, had cast one hasty glance at Astorre he would have paused in amazement, for the monk's face was positively transfigured with sympathy and pity.

But he went on heedless. "When the tyrant at the chase rides past Olympia's house, she rushes to the window and expects to see him dismount at her threshold, and, after this long and sufficient purification by suffering, that he will graciously and kindly conduct her back to court; a thing he really has not the faintest idea of ever doing. Another day, or perhaps, the very same day, she imagines herself banished and persecuted by Ezzelin, who simply does not trouble himself about her.

"She believes herself impoverished, and her estates, which he has never meddled with, confiscated. Thus, she burns and freezes, flying from one extreme to another, is not only distracted herself, but distracts whoever she draws into the whirlpool of her ideas, and is the cause of mischief, where the people believe in her, since being only half a fool, she says many caustic and witty things. To bring her among sensible people, or to a festival, is not to be thought of. It is a miracle that her child Antiope, whom she idolizes, and whose marriage is the aim of all her fancies, has been able to

retain her reason amid such bewildering circumstances, but the girl is in the bloom and
strength of youth, is pretty enough, and has
a sweet nature." So Ascanio rambled on
with his story.

Astorre was lost in dreams! I say this
for what is the past but a dream? All the
monk had experienced three years ago was
before his eyes. He saw a block, the executioner beside it, and he himself, as substitute
for a brother who was ill, waiting to administer the last pious sacrament and give spiri-
tual consolation to some poor sinner. The
prisoner, Count Canossa, at last appeared in
chains, but at the same time seeming far
from prepared to submit to his fate; either
he fancied his pardon was at hand, now that
he stood before the block, or he loved life
and the sun, and abhorred the thought of
darkness and the grave. He treated the
monk rudely and refused to listen to his
prayers. A horrible struggle was impending
if he continued to resist, for he held his child
by the hand, who, unperceived by the
guards, had sprung to his side, and now
clung to him, fastening her expressive eyes,

full of supplication, on the face of the monk. The father drew the child close to his breast, as if with this fresh young life to protect himself from destruction, but was forced down by the executioner and his head pressed upon the block.

Then the child laid her little head beside her father's. Did she hope to awaken the sympathy of the executioner? Did she hope to encourage her father to endure the unavoidable? Was she trying to whisper the name of a Saint in the ear of the unreconciled man? Was she in her overflowing child-like love, without thought or consideration, doing an unheard-of thing? Would she simply die with him?

The vision grew so clear to the mental eye of Astorre as to bring palpably before him, in colors startlingly life-like, the two necks lying side by side. The Count's brown and sunburnt. The child's, white as snow, half-hidden in her golden locks. The little neck was slender and exquisitely formed. Astorre shuddered, lest the falling axe, should mistake its victim, and was stirred to his inmost soul, just as he had been two years before, when the frightful scene actually occurred, although he did not wholly lose consciousness as at the time it happened; then he recovered his senses only after all was over.

"Has my master any commands to give!" and the droning voice of the Majordomo broke in upon his reverie — for this worthy did not at all relish being under Ascanio's orders.

"Burcardo," replied Astorre, in a gentle voice — "do not forget to invite the two ladies Canossa — mother and daughter. It must not be said that the monk ignores those who are shunned and neglected by the world. I recognise the right of the unfortunate woman (here the Majordomo assented with an easy nod) to be invited and received by me. In her condition it might mortify her deeply to be thus overlooked."

"For Heaven's sake, leave her out" cried Ascanio, "your betrothal is even now, a wild affair enough, and it is just such mad-cap proceedings that excite half-crazy people. Take my word for it, she will, as is her wont, do something incredible, fling some unheard-of remark into the midst of the festivities, which already interest the gossiping Paduans sufficiently."

But Messer Burcardo, who believed in the propriety of inviting the Canossa, in the Assembly of the twelve, whether she was in her senses or not, and also that his obedience was due to the Vicedomini and nobody else, bowed low before the monk and said as he withdrew: "Your Lordship alone is to be obeyed."

"Oh, Monk! Monk!" exclaimed Ascanio, "to think of practising divine mercy in a world where common kindness can scarcely be exercised with impunity!"

"Such is human nature," interposed Dante. "A prophetic light sometimes reveals the brink of an abyss, but our imagined cleverness steps in and with smiles and sophistries persuades us there is no danger."

To allay his fears the light-hearted fellow reasoned with himself in this wise. "What in the world is this foolish woman to the monk, in whose life she does not play the slightest part? and after all if she gives us something to laugh at, a spice is added to the Amerella!" He had not the faintest suspicion what was passing in the soul of Astorre, and the monk would never have committed any part of his tender secret to this frivolous worldling.

Therefore Ascanio let well enough alone, and remembering the other command of the tyrant to instruct the monk in the ways of the world enquired cheerily; "Have you thought of the wedding ring Astorre? for it stands written in the 'Ceremonies': section second, paragraph so-and-so, "The rings shall be exchanged." The monk replied he would hunt up one among the family jewels.

"No, indeed, Astorre," said Ascanio, "if you take my advice you will buy your Diana a new one. Who knows what stories may be attached to a ring which has been used? Leave the past entirely behind! Moreover you have now the best opportunity. Go, and buy her a ring of the Florentine on the bridge. Do you know the man? — yet how should you? Listen! early this morning as I was crossing the bridge on foot with Germano

(the crowd was so thick that we had been
obliged to dismount and lead our horses) I
saw, my dear fellow, that at the weather-
beaten head of the pier a goldsmith had
opened his shop and all Padua was haggling
and chaffering over his jewels. And why
on the bridge, do you ask, Astorre, when
there are so many more convenient places?
Because in Florence all the jewelry shops
are on the Arno bridge. Then, (admire the
logic of fashion,) where should one buy his
jewelry if not of a Florentine and where
should a Florentine sell it if not on a bridge?
He would never think of doing differently;
if he does, his wares are always suspected of
being coarse and common, and in fact, he
himself of being no genuine Florentine.
But there's no mistake as to this man. He
has written in enormous letters over his
booth, " Niccolo Lippo dei Lippi, the goldsmith, exiled from his home by one of those
corrupt and unjust decrees but too common
on the Arno. Come, Astorre, let us go to
the bridge."

Astorre did not refuse. He may himself
have felt the need of breaking the spell of

isolation which had bound him to the house
ever since he threw off the monk's garb.

" Have you any money in your pocket? "
asked Ascanio jokingly, " remember your
vow of poverty is broken and the Florentine
will charge you enough." The monk rapped
on a window-pane in the room of the house-
steward, conveniently situated on the lower
floor over which the young men were now
passing; the cunning face of the steward
instantly appeared (a Genoese, if I've been
rightly informed) and with a fawning bow
he reached his master a purse well-filled with
Byzantine gold. A servant then enveloped
the monk in a comfortable summer mantle
with a large hood.

Upon the street, Astorre drew the hood
deep over his face, less on account of the
burning rays of the sun, than· from long
habit, and turning to his companion said
pleasantly, " Am I not to be trusted to go
alone on this small errand, Ascanio ? Surely
to buy a simple gold ring is not beyond the
capacity of a monk, you'll risk me so far, *a
rivederci* when the vesper bell rings." Ascanio left him and called back over his

shoulder "One, not two, Diana gives you yours, remember that Astorre." 'Twas only one of the many light bubbles which the merry fellow blew into the air every day.

"If you ask me, Prince, why the monk dismissed his friend, I answer, that he longed to let the heavenly chords ring out clear and full which the child martyr had awakened in his soul."

Astorre had reached the bridge. Notwithstanding the burning heat of the sun, it was crowded with people, and from both shores a double line of men and women were passing before the shop of the Florentine. The monk was not recognized under his cloak, although now and again a questioning eye rested upon the uncovered part of his face. Nobles and citizens pressed around the booth. High-born dames alighted from their chairs and consented to be squeezed and jostled for the sake of buying a pair of bracelets or a coronet of the latest pattern. By the ringing of a bell, the Florentine had announced everywhere that he should close to-day after the *Ave Maria*. He had never dreamed of doing anything

of the sort, but what does a lie cost a
Florentine?

At last the monk stood before the booth,
closely hemmed in by the crowd. The besieged trader who seemed to multiply himself
tenfold glanced at the monk and at once
detected his inexperience. "How can I
serve the cultivated taste of Eccellenza?" he
asked. "Give me a simple gold ring,"
replied the monk. The merchant seized a
cup exquisitely wrought and covered with
reliefs in Florentine taste, and shaking the
bowl which contained more than a hundred
rings offered it to Astorre.

The monk now found himself in a state
of painful embarassment, he had no idea of
the size of the finger on which he was to
put the ring and, taking up several, hesitated
whether to buy a large or a small one. The
Florentine could not repress a gibe, for it
was the fashion on the Arno to add a sting
to every speech. "Does not Eccellenza
know the size of the finger he has pressed
so often?" he enquired, with innocent mien,
yet, like the shrewd man he was, correcting
himself instantly as he remembered that

most men preferred being thought knaves
than fools, gave Astorre two rings, a large
and a small one, which he contrived to slip
between the thumb and forefinger of the
monk: "for the Signor's two loves," he
whispered, bowing.

Before the monk, however, could manifest
his indignation at this impudent remark he
received a violent blow.   It was the shoulder-
piece of a horse in armor, which struck him
so hard that he let the small ring fall to the
ground.   At the same moment the deafen-
ing blast of eight trumpets sounded in his
ears.   The band of the governor's German
body-guard was riding in two lines of four
horses each over the bridge, shoving the
crowd in all directions and pressing the
people up against the stone parapet.

The old wooden planks of the bridge
were much worn, and, especially in the
middle, full of ruts, into one of which the
ring fell, and rolled over to the other side.
Here a young maid named Isotta (or, as
they shorten the name in Padua, Sotte)
snatched up the sparkling thing, at the im-
minent risk of being trampled on by the

horses. " A lucky ring ! " shouted the silly
girl and with childish glee forced it on to
the slender finger of her young mistress,
whom she was accompanying ; it was the'
fourth finger of her left hand, which by its
delicate shape, seemed to her especially
worthy of this pretty ornament. In Padua,
as in Verona, if I am right, they wear the
betrothal-ring on the left hand.

The noble Signorina was annoyed at
Sotte's joke and yet somewhat amused by it.
She struggled hard to pull the strange ring
off again, but it resisted her efforts as if it
had been molded on. Suddenly the monk
stood before her in an attitude of joyful surprise. He had laid his left hand over his
heart while his right was extended toward
her, for although she had attained the
bloom of maidenhood, by the exquisite deli-
cacy of her throat, and still more by the
beating of his own heart, he had recognized
the child whose tender head he last saw on
the block.

Whilst the young girl stood confused,
now lifting her questioning eyes to the
monk and then letting them fall upon the

refractory ring, Astorre hesitated to ask
her for it, still it had to be done. He
opened his lips; "Signorina" he began and
felt himself in the embrace of two strong
mailed arms, which had taken possession of
him bodily. In a moment with the help of
another soldier he was seated astride an
impatient steed. "Let us see," laughed a
good-natured voice, "whether you have forgotten how to ride." It was Germano, at
the head of the German cohort, which the
Governor had ordered out for a review in the
plain near Padua. Meeting his brother-in-
law in this unexpected manner on the bridge
he had conceived the joke of mounting him
on one of the horses from which a young
Swabian sprang off at his command. The
fiery steed, detecting instantly the change of
riders, made a couple of wild springs; it
caused a stampede on the crowded bridge,
and Astorre, whose hood had fallen back,
and who, with difficulty kept hold of the
reins, was recognized by the startled people.
"The Monk! The Monk!" resounded from
all sides, but the martial troop had already
left the bridge and soon disappeared round

the corner of the street. The Florentine,
who was left unpaid, rushed after him. He
had scarcely gone twenty steps, however,
when he turned back, afraid to leave his
wares under the slight protection of a small
boy, and besides, the cries of the multitude
warned him that he had to deal with some
one well known in the city who could be
easily hunted up. He had Astorre's palace
pointed out to him and presented himself
there that same day, the following, and the
day after. The two first days he could get
no answer to his questions, for the monk's
household was turned upside down, the
third he found the tyrant's seal affixed to the
closed door; this frightened the coward and
he went off without his pay.

Meanwhile the women, Antiope, the giddy
maid, and a third, who, separated from them
by the tumult on the bridge, had now re-
joined them, started off in an opposite
direction. This third was an odd-looking,
prematurely aged woman, with deeply fur-
rowed brow and gray bushy locks, She had
an excited air as she dragged her untidy,
but still aristocratic dress, through the dust
of the streets.

With foolish exultation Sotte instantly related to the elderly lady, evidently the mother of the damsel; the occurrence on the bridge. Astorre, she also had recognized him by the cries of the people. Astorre, the monk, whose wooing was the talk of the town, had surreptitiously rolled to the feet of Antiope a gold ring, and when she, Sotte, perceiving the hand of Fate, and the cunning of the monk, had put the ring on the dear girl's hand, the monk himself had stept up to them and, when Antiope modestly wished to return the ring, had laid his left hand tenderly on his heart — here she imitated the monk raising his right hand in refusal, with a gesture which in all Italy says, and signifies, " Keep it, my dear!"

At last the astounded Antiope found a chance to say a word for herself, and besought her mother to pay no heed to Sotte's nonsense, but in vain. Signora Olympia raised her hands toward Heaven, and in the open streets thanked St. Anthony with fervor for having listened to her daily prayer, beyond all hopes or expectations, in that he had bestowed upon her darling one of his own

sons, a well-born virtuous man.. She accompanied all this with such extravagant gesticu-
lation that the passers-by laughed and tapped
their foreheads. The bewildered Antiope
tried in all conceivable ways to reason her
mother out of the delusion; the elderly
Canossa refused to listen, and went on passionately building up her air-castle.

When the ladies reached the Canossa
palace they were met in the arched door-way
by a stiffly attired Majordomo followed by
six gorgeously dressed servants. Messer
Burcardo stept back respectfully to allow
Madonna Olympia to ascend the stairs first.
Entering one of the deserted halls he made
three measured bows, each one deeper than
the last, and bringing him a little nearer to
the ladies, when he said slowly and with
great solemnity: " Illustrissimi, Astorre
Vicedomini sends me to invite you most
humbly to his espousals this evening (he
repressed with bitterness " in ten days ") at
the ringing of the vesper bell." —

Dante paused. Abundance of material for
his romance lay before him but his severe
taste led him to wish to simplify and arrange
it.

"My Dante," said Cangrande, "I admire the strong clear-cut outlines with which you have drawn your Florentines. Niccolo Lippo dei Lippi was banished from Florence by a corrupt and unrighteous decree, but he himself is an extortioner, flatterer, liar, scoffer, cheat and coward, all after the manner of the Florentines. But this is only a faint shower compared with that fiery rain of denunciation which you have poured down on your beloved city, only one last drop of the gall and vinegar which you have given to the Florentines in some parts of your Commedia. Let me tell you it is ignoble to defame one's birthplace and to give your own mother cause to blush. It is not becoming. It does not make a good impression.

I will tell you of a puppet show which I saw the other day, while going about disguised among my people. You are perhaps shocked to hear that I have such low taste as to enjoy puppets and fools in my leisure moments. Yet imagine yourself standing with me before the little stage. What do you see? A man and his wife quarreling.

He whips her and she weeps. A neighbor puts his head in at the door, scolds the man, rebukes him, in short, interferes. But lo! the brave wife raises up against the intruder and takes the part of her husband. "What if it is my pleasure to be whipped," she sobs.

Even so, my Dante, a noble-spirited man if ill-treated by his father-land still says "What if it is my pleasure to be whipped?"

Many young keen eyes were directed upon the Florentine. He remained silent, with bowed head. What was passing in his mind no one knew, but when he raised his face again his brow was sadder, his mouth sterner and more severe. He listened. The wind howled round the turrets of the castle and blew open a loosely-fastened shutter in the apartment where the party were sitting. Monte Baldo had sent its first cold blast. They saw the flakes whirling about in the air lighted up by the fire on the hearth. The poet gazed at the snow-storm, and his days, which he felt were gliding away, seemed to him like these white flakes, hunted and driven through the air, lighted up only now and then by an unsteady gleam. He shivered with cold.

And his sympathetic listeners realized, as he did, that no true home, but only the uncertain favor of fickle patrons protected him from the storms of winter which were sweeping over fields and highways.   All felt, but none more than Cangrande, whose spirit was indeed great and noble,—here sits a homeless wanderer.

The Prince rose and shaking the fool like a feather from his mantle, went up to the exiled man and took him by the hand, and as he gave him his own place near the fire said, " This seat is yours, by right!" Dante did not gainsay it.   Cangrande himself took possession of the empty stool. Here he could comfortably observe the two ladies, between whom the wanderer through the Inferno now sat.   The firelight shone upon him, and he continued his story as follows : —

" While the vesper bells in Padua were sounding, there assembled under the stately rafters of the Vicedomini·hall all the members that remained of the twelve noble families.   They awaited the coming of the master of the house.   Diana stood beside

her father and brother. A low murmur of
talk went on. The men discussed gravely
the political effect of this union of two great
city families. The young people joked in
an undertone over the idea of a married
monk. The older ladies shuddered, in spite
of the Pope's letter, at the sacrilege, and
only those surrounded by growing daughters
were disposed to regard it in a milder light
and find excuses on the plea of the ex- -
traordinary pressure of circumstances, or
the tender-heartedness of the monk. The
maidens were one and all aglow with expec-
tation.

The presence of Olympia Canossa caused
wonder and uneasiness, for she was showily
dressed, in regal style, as if prepared
to take a prominent part in the approaching ceremony, and was now talking with
strange eagerness and volubility to her
daughter Antiope, who endeavoured, though
apparently in vain, to calm her by whispered
entreaties and caresses. Madonna Olympia
had already been considerably offended on
the stairs where, Messer Burcardo being
occupied with the reception of two other

noble families, they had been greeted by Gocciola, holding most respectfully his new scarlet cap with the silver bells in his hands. She frightened or annoyed the other guests by her extravagant gesticulations. The poor creature was pointed at by everybody. No one else in the monk's place would ever have thought of inviting her, and they all felt sure she would play them one of her mad pranks.

Messer Burcardo announced his lord. In the afternoon Astorre having freed himself as soon as possible, from Germano, had returned to the bridge, where of course, neither the ring nor the ladies were to be found. He overwhelmed himself with reproaches, although in truth, chance only was to blame, and in the hours which remained to him before vespers, he framed the resolve to behave more circumspectly in future. Filled with this determination he now entered the hall and stept into the midst of the assembly. The consciousness of being the object of general attention and the constraint and demands of society which he felt, so to speak, in the air, suggested to him that the bare truth, strong and hateful as it was, could not be spoken, but that he must give it a milder and more pleasing aspect. He instinctively struck the mean between truth and conventionality and spoke as follows: —

" Noble friends and fellow kinsmen : death has reaped a rich harvest among us Vicedomini. As I stand before you clothed in black I wear mourning for my father, three brothers and three nephews. Set free by the church, after mature deliberation and conscientious weighing of the matter before God (here his voice grew husky), I felt that I could not disregard or leave unfulfilled the wish of a dying father to perpetuate his race. You will judge this act of mine according to the justice and clemency inherent in you and either approve or condemn me. But in one point you will all agree, that, considering my past life it would have ill become me to hesitate and choose, and that only such a union could be pleasing in the sight of God as offered itself most naturally.

With whom could it seem more natural to form a lasting bond, than with this young widow to whom I am already united by my inconsolable grief for the loss of my dear brother? Therefore I took this hand over the deathbed of my dear father, as I take it now,"—he stepped up to Diana, led her into the centre of the room, — "and I put on her finger the betrothal ring."

It was done. The ring fitted. Diana likewise put a ring on the monk's finger. " It belonged to my mother," she said, " who was a true and virtuous wife. I give thee a ring which has kept troth." A ceremonious murmur of congratulation, from all present, closed the solemn act, and the aged Pizziguerra, a hale, white-haired old man, for avarice does not shorten one's existence, wept the usual tear.

Madonna Olympia saw her dream castle burst into flames and burn with crackling timbers and falling pillars. She took one step forward as if to convince herself that her eyes were not deceiving her, then another, becoming ever wilder, and now she stood directly before Astorre and Diana, her gray hair bristling, while mad words, like the cries of an infuriated mob, poured from her lips.

" Wretch!" she shrieked, "against the ring on the finger of this lady protests another,

and the one which was first given." She
grasped Antiope, who had followed her with
increasing anxiety, drew her forward and
raised the young girl's hand as she said,
" This ring you put on the finger of my child
near the shop of the Florentine upon the
bridge not an hour ago : " for thus had she
shaped the facts in her disordered brain.
" Infamous man ! Treacherous monk ! why
does not the earth open and swallow you ?
We will hang the porter of your cloister, who
snored over his pipe, and let you escape from
your cell. If you would follow your guilty
passions you might choose another prey than
an unjustly persecuted, lonely widow, and an
unprotected orphan.

The marble floor did not open, and the
poor unhappy woman, who thought she was
expressing her just indignation very mildly,
read in the eyes of the guests surrounding her
outright scorn, or pity of a wholly different
kind from that which she had expected. She
heard behind her whispered clearly the word
" fool," and her rage burst out in crazy laugh.
ter. " Who is the fool here ? " she asked
with a scornful sneer ; " who, but a fool,

could choose so stupidly between these two?
I make you judges, you Signors and all who
have eyes. Here is a charming little head
and the fresh beauty of youth "; — the rest I
have forgotten — only this hint I remember
distinctly, that among the young men, more
than one might have been a rake. All
the youths — those who were virtuous and
those who were not — closed their eyes and
ears to the excited behaviour of a mother who
was trampling under foot the modesty and
reputation of the child that she had borne.

Everybody in the hall pitied Antiope, except Diana who, though far from doubting
the monk's truth, felt a species of resentment
toward the beauty, so boldly paraded before
her bridegroom.

Antiope may have done wrong in keeping
the ring on her finger, perhaps she did it in
order not to irritate farther her already
distracted mother, and hoping the poor
woman when undeceived by the reality,
would, as usual, come down from her high
horse, and after a few resentful glances and
murmured words, resign herself to the inevi-
table; or perhaps the young Antiope had

herself dipped a finger in the bubbling fairy spring. Was not the meeting on the bridge strange indeed, and if she should be proved to have been the monk's choice, would it be more remarkable than the fate which had torn him from the cloister?

But if this was the case she now suffered a most cruel punishment. Her own mother had soiled her fair fame by unlicensed speech.

A deep blush, and a still deeper, covered her face and neck, then, in the general silence she began to weep loud and bitterly.

At this even the gray-haired Mænad stopped and listened. Then a frightful pain seemed to convulse her face and her rage increased. "And this other" she shrieked, pointing to Diana, "this broad piece of marble, scarcely hewed out of the rough, this ill-made giantess, which the Almighty Father formed when he was still an apprentice just: learning to knead the dough, fie! fie! on this bungled clumsy body without life and soul, for who could have given her a soul? her bastard mother, the stupid Ossola? or that niggardly miser there? Only with reluctance has he given her the barest apology for one."

The old Pizziguèrra stood perfectly un-
moved; with the clear understanding of a
miser he did not forget whom he had before
him. But his daughter Diana forgot it.
Beside herself, at the rude insult offered her,
she frowned terribly, and clenched her hands,
but, when the crazy woman attacked her
parents, insulted her mother in the grave,
and held up her father to general contempt,
she lost all trace of self-control.

"Hound!" she exclaimed, and struck Antiope in the face, for the loving and coura-
geous girl had thrown herself before her
mother; Antiope uttered a cry which rang
through the hall and thrilled to the heart
every one present.

The wheel in the head of the poor crazy
woman turned completely round. Her wild
fury changed into piteous wailing. "They
have beaten my child" she groaned, sank
upon her knees and sobbed, "is there no
longer any God in Heaven?"

With this the measure was full. It
would have run over earlier, but that Fate
rushed on quicker than my tongue could
relate it, so quick indeed that neither the

monk, nor Germano standing close beside
her saw Diana's uplifted arm in time to
seize and restrain it. Ascanio grasped the
mad woman round the waist, one of his
friends took her by the feet and, scarcely
resisting, she was carried out of the hall, put
into her chair, and taken home.

Diana and Antiope remained standing
face to face, one whiter than the other;
Diana, contrite and repentant after her
sudden fit of passion; Antiope struggling
for words,— her lips moved, but no sound
escaped them.

If the monk now seized Antiope's hand to
give his escort to her, who had been so mal-
treated by his betrothed wife, he only fulfilled
his chivalrous and hospitable duty. Everybody understood this. Diana, too, must
surely desire to have the victim of her violence
withdrawn from her sight. After a little
while she departed with her father and brother,
and the assembled guests likewise left as
quickly as possible.

There came a sound from under the table
loaded with Cyprian wine and Amarella. A
fool's cap appeared and Gocciola crept on all

fours out of his agreeable hiding-place. In his view the course things had taken was only too delightful, since now he had full freedom to gorge himself with Amarella, and to empty one glass after another. Thus he revelled for a time until he heard steps approaching. His first impulse was to fly, but casting an angry look on the intruder he deemed flight unnecessary. It was the monk returning to his princely home joyous, exultant, and quite as intoxicated as himself, ·for the monk —"

"Loved Antiope," interrupted the Prince's fair friend with a forced laugh.

"You have said it, lady," responded the narrator in a tragic tone, "he loved Antiope."

"Naturally." "How else?" "It must be so!" "'Tis the usual way!" resounded from all sides.

"Softly, young people," murmured Dante. "No, 'tis not the usual way. Do you think then that a love which implies the surrender of life and soul is an everyday affair? And do you really imagine that you have or are loving in this way? Undeceive yourselves. Everyone talks of spirits but few have seen

them. I will give you an indisputable proof
of this. There is lying about in the house
here a much-read storybook. Skimming
through it I discovered amid plenty of rub-
bish one true word. " Love," says this book,
" is rare, and generally comes to a bad end."
Thus much Dante had said in all seriousness,
then he went on playfully. " Since you are
all so thoroughly versed in love, and especially since it does not fall within my province
to instruct the young from my worthless
head in such matters, I will pass by the
treacherous soliloquy of the monk and say
briefly that when the sensible Ascanio overheard it, he was alarmed and tried to reason
with him."

" Will you mutilate your touching romance
in this way, noble Dante ? " said the excited
friend of the Prince, as she turned toward
the Florentine with imploring hands. "Pray,
let us hear what the monk says, that our
sympathy may be with him as we see him
turn from a rough to a delicate nature ; from
a cold and stormy heart, to one that is warm
and full of feeling."

" Yes, Florentine," interrupted the Prin-

cess with burning cheeks, "let your monk
speak that we may hear with amazement
how it was that Astorre, however inexperienced, and easily duped, could have been
tempted to leave a noble woman for a wily
flirt; for have you not perceived that Antiope is a flirt? You know women little, however. In truth I assure you," she raised her
powerful arm and rolled her fist—"that, I
too would have struck, not the poor crazy
woman, but, deliberately, the cunning flirt,
who was determined at any cost to attract to
herself the attention of the monk," and she
struck the blow in the air. The friend of
the Prince trembled.

Cangrande, who never took his eyes off
the two ladies sitting opposite him, admired
this display of passion on the part of his
Princess. He found her, at that moment,
incomparably more beautiful than the delicate little rival he had given her; the highest and deepest feelings only come to full
expression in a strong body and powerful
soul.

Dante, on his side, smiled, for the first
and only time during this evening, as he saw

the two ladies contending so sharply over
the action of his story. He even conde-
scended to a touch of raillery.

" Princesses," said he, " what do you demand of me? Soliloquy is irrational: Does
a wise man ever talk to himself? "

A saucy, curly-haired page now started up
from behind a chair and cried: " How little,
great Master, are you aware of what you
have asserted! Know, Dante, that nobody
talks more earnestly and volubly to himself
than you. To such a degree indeed that you
not only overlook stupid boys like myself,
but, let even beauty pass disregarded."

" Really," replied Dante, " where was that
and when? " " Yesterday upon the bridge,"
said the boy, smiling. " You were leaning
upon its stone railing. The charming Lucre-
zia Nani passed by, almost touching your
toga. We boys followed, admiring her, and
two fiery soldiers hurried on to catch one
glance from her soft eyes. She, however,
sought yours, for not everyone has wandered
at will through the Inferno. But you were
watching the waves in the river, and murmuring something to yourself."

" I was sending a greeting to the far ocean.
The waves were more beautiful than the
maiden. Let us return to the two fools.
And by all the Muses interrupt me no more,
else midnight will find me still in the midst
of the story."

"When the monk after leading Antiope
home re-entered his hall — I forgot to say
that he had not met Ascanio, although his
friend had gone the same way in convey-
ing Madonna Olympia to her castle — but as
soon as Ascanio had committed the lady into
the hands of her servants he had hastened
to his uncle, the tyrant, that he might retail
to him the whole affair as the last joke.
He would ten times rather any day inform
Ezzelin of a city scandal than of a conspiracy.
I know not whether the monk really was as
handsome as Ascanio painted him, but I see
him enter his hall radiant with the flush of
youth and as if borne onward by the zephyrs
with flying feet that skimmed the ground.
His eyes are full of sunlight and he murmurs
rapturous words. Gocciola who had drunk
a great deal of Cyprian wine likewise felt

happy and rejuvenated, under his feet also the marble floor resolved itself into a white cloud. He felt an unconquerable thirst to catch the words as they fell from Astorre's fresh lips and began to measure the length of the hall beside him, half-striding, half-skipping, the fool's sceptre under his arm.

"The loving head, once offered for the father, has again made a sacrifice of itself for the mother," murmured Astorre, "Those delicate cheeks, how they tingled under the insult! the poor abused maiden, how her cries wrung all our hearts! Has she ever been out of my thoughts since she lay on the block? She has dwelt in my soul. She has accompanied me, present everywhere, floating through my prayers, beaming in my cell, her head upon my pillow. The darling head with the slender little white neck, did I not see it even beside that of St. Paul!

"Of St. Paul?" giggled the fool "of the St. Paul in our altar picture, with the rough black hair, and the red neck on the low broad block and the executioner's axe over it?" Gocciola sometimes performed his devotions in the Franciscan church.

The monk nodded. " When I gazed at it long the axe seemed to quiver and I shuddered. Have I not confessed this to the prior ? "

" And what did the prior say ? " enquired Gocciola.

" My son " said he, " what you saw was a child heralding the triumphant procession of the heavenly hosts. Fear not; to that ambrosial neck, no harm can come."

" But " insinuated the wicked fool, " the child has grown up. So high ! " He raised his hand, then bringing it gradually down nearly to the ground, grinned, " and the cowl of your lordship has dropt so low."

Vulgarity could not touch the monk. From Antiope's hand he had caught a creative spark which now began to glow in his veins, at first mildly and tenderly, but soon more and more fiercely until it overmastered him completely and obliterated all considerations. " Praised be the Lord Almighty " he burst out joyfully, "who has created man and woman."

" Eve ? " asked the fool.

" Antiope " replied the monk.

"And the other one, the tall one, what will you do with her? Will you send her a-begging?" and Gocciola wiped his eyes.

"What other?" asked the monk. "Is there any other beside Antiope?"

This was too much even for the fool. He stared at the monk with open mouth, but was suddenly seized by a hand on his collar, dragged toward the door and dropped on the pavement. The same hand was then laid on Astorre's shoulder. "Wake up, dreamer!" cried Ascanio, who had returned and heard the monk's last ecstatic speech. He drew the enthusiast down upon the window-seat, looked him straight in the eyes, and said, "Astorre you are out of your senses."

The monk at first lowered his eyes before this searching look, as if blinded by it, then for a moment met it with his own, full of rapture and said in a quiet tone, "Do you wonder?"

"As little as I would at the kindling of a flame," replied Ascanio. "Since however, you are not a blind element but a reason and a will, trample out the flame else it will consume you and all Padua. Must a child of

the world teach you the Divine and Human
law? You are betrothed. This ring on
your finger declares it. If you, having first
broken your vow, now break your engagement, you war against custom, duty, honor,
and the peace of the city. If you do not
quickly and heroically draw out of your heart
the arrow of the blind god, it will kill you,
Antiope, and a few others, who may chance
to be in its way. Astorre! Astorre!"

Ascanio's merry lips were astonished at
the great and earnest words, which, in the
anguish of his heart, he gave them to utter.
"Thy good name Astorre," he added half
jokingly, "brays like a trumpet, calling thee
to fight against thyself."

Astorre mastered himself. "They have
given me a philter," he exclaimed. "I rave,
I am crazy. Ascanio, I give myself into thy
power,— Chain me!"

"I will chain you to Diana," said Ascanio,
"follow me that we may find her."

"Was it not Diana who struck Antiope?"
asked the monk.

"Oh, you have dreamed the whole thing,
you were out of your senses. Come, I con-

jure you, nay, command you. I take you by
force and lead you." .

If Ascanio had wished to chase away the
ugly truth, the clinking sound of Germano's
heels upon the floor brought it all back.
With resolute face Diana's brother came up
to the monk and seized his hand saying:
" A disturbed feast, brother-in-law. My sister
sends me — no, I deceive you — she did not
send me for she has locked herself up in her
chamber and there she sits bemoaning and
cursing her violence ; to-day we are drowned
in women's tears. She loves thee, but cannot bring it over her lips to say so, it is in
our family, I cannot say such things either.
She has never for an instant doubted thee.
The explanation is simple — You have by
accident lost a ring, or flung it away, if it
was yours, which the little Canossa (what is
her name), Antiope, had on her finger. The
crazy mother found it and spun this yarn
about it. Antiope is, of course, as innocent
as a new-born babe, of the whole affair,—
who says otherwise must answer to me."

" Not I," cried Astorre. " Antiope is pure
as an angel. The ring rolled to her feet by

chance," and he went on with hurried words to explain the matter.

" But, my sister's action, can you find no excuse for that, Astorre?" pleaded Germano. " The blood rushed to her head and she did not see whom she had before her. She meant to strike the mad woman who had insulted her parents, and hit instead this dear innocent girl. She must be restored to honor and respect before God and man. Let this be my duty, brother-in-law,— I am her brother — it is simple."

" You speak with assurance, Germano, but your meaning is not clear. What do you propose? How will you make amends to the poor girl?" asked Ascanio.

" It is simple," repeated Germano. " I will offer Antiope Canossa my hand, and will make her my wife."

Ascanio put his hand to his brow. The proposal almost stunned him. As he rapidly considered and looked at it more closely, the heroic resource did not seem to him so bad, but he cast an anxious look at the monk. Astorre, master of himself once more maintained absolute silence and listened attentively. The soldier's fine sense of honor, with his directness, seemed to echo and re-echo like a clear call through the desert of his soul.

" Thus I can hit two birds with one stone, Brother-in-law," explained Germano. " The maiden is reinstated in her honor and chastity. I should like to see who would whisper behind my wife's back, and I make peace between you two married people. Diana no longer needs to feel ashamed and mortified before you, or before herself, and is at the same time thoroughly cured of her violent temper. She is cured of it for life, I assure you."

Astorre pressed his hand. " You are a brave honest man," he said. The determination to overcome his own earthly, or heavenly passion strengthened in him. Yet this resolve was not free, and this virtue not unselfish, for it was attached to a dangerous sophism, viz : — " as I embrace an unloved woman, Antiope will be embraced by an un-loved man, who marries her off-hand to make reparation for another's fault ; penance and renunciation are everywhere in the world as in the cloister."

"What must be done, I propose shall not be delayed," urged Germano, "else she will toss about all night without sleep," (I do not know whether he meant Diana, or Antiope). "Brother-in-law, go with me as witness, we will do it in proper form."

"No, no," cried Ascanio, frightened, "not Astorre: take me!"

Germano shook his head, "Ascanio, my friend, you are not suited for this. You are not a sufficiently grave witness in affairs of marriage. Moreover, my brother, Astorre would not let anybody else woo for me. It is indeed to a great extent his own matter. Is it not Astorre?" The monk bowed. "Prepare then directly, Brother-in-law. Make yourself fine. Throw a gold chain over your dress."

"And," said Ascanio, with a forced laugh, "as you pass through the court dip your head in the fountain."

"But you, Germano, are in such warlike armor! is it suited for wooing?"

"It is long since I have been out of armor, and it becomes me. Why are you looking at me, with such scrutiny, from head to foot, Ascanio?"

" I am asking myself whence this mailed knight derives his assurance that he will not be pitched into the moat together with his scaling ladder? "

" There can be no question in this case," tranquilly opined Germano "will she, insulted and beaten, as she has been, refuse the hand of a knight? If so, she is a greater fool than her mother — that is clear as the sun, Ascanio. Come, Astorre! "

Whilst with folded arms the friend thus left behind reflected on the new turn things had taken, questioning whether it led to a play-ground for happy children or to the Campo Santo, his young companions walked across the piazza which divided them from ths Canossa palace.

The cloudless day was dying in a sunset of molten gold, and the *Ave* was ringing. The monk repeated to himself the usual prayer, and the chimes of the cloister, which stood somewhat high, prolonged the familiar sound by a few sad peaceful strokes after the city bells were hushed. The monk was conscious of sharing in the universal peace.

Just then his eyes were attracted to the

face of his friend and rested on his weather-hardened features. They were lighted up with the joy of duty fulfilled beyond question, but more still by the unconscious, or unconsciously manifest happiness at reaching the port of a blessed island under sails filled with the breath of honor and of chivalrous action. "The sweet innocent!" sighed the soldier!

With the speed of lightning the idea shot through Astorre's brain that Diana's brother deceived himself if he thought he was acting from disinterested motives. On the contrary Germano loved Antiope, and was his rival. He felt a sharp pang, and then one still sharper, until he could have shrieked, and a whole nest of furious snakes seemed writhing and raging in his bosom. May God protect us all, both men and women, from jealousy! It is the most insidious of the passions, and who suffers it is more damned than any inhabitant of hell.

With suffocating heart and a face tortured by dismay the monk followed the self-confident wooer up the steps of the palace they had now reached. It was empty and

and will stand by Germano during his wooing. On the topmost stair he invoked all the Saints, especially St. Francis the master of self-conquest. He clutched his breast, and believed by heavenly aid, that, strong as Hercules, he had strangled the serpents. But the Saint, with the four stigmas, turned a deaf ear to his faithless disciple, who had forsworn rope and cowl.

Germano, in the meantime, was sketching out his speech, but could get no farther than the two arguments which dawned upon him at the outset. He was, however, full of splendid courage, had often addressed his Germans, before a cavalry encounter and would not now allow himself to be daunted by a maiden. Only this waiting was unbearable. He clanked his sword.

Antiope started, looked up, rose quickly and stood with her back toward the window, turning a face full of wonder and sadness upon the two men who were bowing before her.

" Be comforted Antiope Canossa," said Germano, addressing her. " I bring with me as legal witness this man Astorre Vice. domini, whom they call the monk, the spouse of my sister Diana; I have come to ask you, as you are without a father, and with such a mother, to give yourself to me as my wife. My sister has forgotten her true self in her treatment of you," — he would not use a stronger term, and thus compromise Diana, whom he revered — "and I, her brother, am here to offer restitution for the wrong my sister has done. Diana with Astorre, you with me; by this means will you two women be brought together again, and persuaded to join hands in loving friendship."

The sensitive spirit of the monk was stung by this rude speech, which placed the aggressor on equal footing with the aggrieved one, or was it a viper writhing in his breast? He whispered to the soldier, " Germano, one does not woo in this way."

His companion heard it, and at the same time receiving no response from Antiope, lost his temper. He felt that he ought to be more gentle, yet spoke even more brusquely than at first, "without a father and having such a mother," he repeated, "you need a manly protector. You might have learned this to-day, Signorina. You cannot wish to be a second time mortified and abused before all Padua. Give yourself to me, as you are, and I will protect you from the crown of your head to the soles of your feet."

Germano was thinking of his armor.

Astorre found this proposal revolting. He thought Germano treated Antiope as if she were his battle-prize, or did a snake hiss once more in his breast? "This is not the way to woo, Germano," he gasped. The soldier turned and replied, " If you under-stand it better, woo for me brother-in-law," and he stept aside to give him his place.

Then Astorre approached and, bending his knee, raised his hands with the palms clasped while with wistful face he gazed at the delicate head on the pale gold background. Does Love find words? Silence seemed to fill the darkening room.

Finally Antiope whispered " For whom dost thou woo, Astorre?" "For this man here, for my brother Germano," came from his pale lips. Then she hid her face in her hands.

Germano lost all patience. " I shall speak plainly with her," he burst out. " In two words, Antiope Canossa, will you be my wife or not ? "

Antiope moved her little head gently and softly, but it was in distinct refusal.

"Well, I have my answer" said Germano, drily, "Come brother-in-law," and he quitted the hall with as firm a step as he had entered it. The monk, however, did not follow him.

Astorre remained in his supplicating attitude, then, trembling, seized Antiope's quivering hands and drew them away from her face. Which mouth sought the other I know not, for it had become perfectly dark in the room; it was so still also that if their ears had not been filled with sounds of rapturous joy the lovers might have heard the prayers murmured in an adjoining apartment. Next to Antiope's room, though some steps below it, was the home chapel, and on the morrow the third anniversary of the death of Count Canossa was there to be solemnized. Immediately after the city bells tolled the hour of midnight, masses for his soul were to be read in presence of the widow and orphaned child. The priest was already on the spot waiting for his assistants.

As little as the subterranean murmur did they hear the shuffling of Madonna Olympia's slippers, who was seeking her daughter and now by the scant light of the house-lantern, which she bore in her hand, was quietly and earnestly watching the lovers. That the boldest lie of an extravagant imagination had become a fact before her eyes, in these tenderly entwined forms, did not astonish Madonna Olympia, nor on the other hand did she feel any revenge toward Diana. She was not revelling in the bitter pangs now in store for the haughty Pizziguerra. Her simple motherly joy at seeing her child justly valued and loved overpowered every other emotion.

When at last, struck by a sharp beam from her lantern, the two looked up surprised, she asked in a tender natural voice, " Astorre Vicedomini, do you love Antiope Canossa? "

" Beyond all else," was his reply. " And will defend her?" "Against a world," he cried boldly. " That is right," she said graciously, " but you mean it honestly, do you not? You will not disown her, as you have done Diana? You are not fooling me!

You will not make a poor distracted creature, as they call me, more unhappy? You will not leave my little girl again to be disgraced? You will not seek for excuses or delays? You will give certainty to my eyes and like brave knight and good Christian lead her at once to the altar. Nor have you far to go, for a priest (do you hear that murmur?) is kneeling at this moment in the chapel down there."

And she opened a low door behind which a few steep stairs led down into the sanctuary. Astorre turned his head; under the rough vault before a small altar, by the flickering light of candles, a bare-footed monk was praying, who in age and stature reminded him of himself, and who also wore the rope and cowl of the order of St. Francis.

I believe that this bare-footed friar must have been sent by Providence to kneel and pray here exactly at this hour in order to warn and frighten Astorre for the last time, but in his burning veins the medicine turned to poison. At sight of this representative of his former life a spirit of defiance and a determination to free himself from rules and restrictions took possession of him.

" At one leap I set myself free from my first vow," he said, derisively, " and saw the barriers fall beneath me, why not do so with the second? My saints have not sustained me in my hour of trial, perhaps they will save and defend the sinner ; " and the bewildered man, clasping Antiope in his arms, bore rather than led her down the steps.

Madonna Olympia, who after a brief interval of reason relapsed into madness, had slammed the heavy door behind the monk and her child, as if it were a trap in which to catch her prey, and was now stopping herself to listen at the key-hole.

What she saw no one knows. It was said later that Astorre, with drawn sword, had threatened and overpowered the Franciscan. This is impossible, for Astorre never girded on a sword in his life. It may be nearer true, sad to say, that the monk was corrupt and that the purse Astorre took with him when he went to buy the wedding-ring for Diana wandered into the pocket of the cowled brother.

But that at first the priest refused, that the two monks wrestled with one another, and that the ponderous vault hid a direful scene, this I read in the convulsed and terrified face of the listener. Donna Olympia understood that a crime of some sort was being committed and that she, as the inciter and accomplice of the same, had exposed herself to the power of the law, and the revenge of the woman who was betrayed. Being already overwrought by the return of the day on which her husband had been beheaded, she imagined that her own crazy head was likewise doomed to the block. She fancied she heard the step of Ezzelin approaching and fled screaming " Help! Murder!"

The distracted woman rushed to the entrance hall where a window looked out upon the narrow inner court. "My mule! My chair!" she cried in the same breath, and her servants, laughing at the double command, since the mule was for the country and the chair for the town, came slowly and leisurely out of a corner, where they had been drinking and gambling by the light of one poor lantern. An old groom who alone remained faithful to his unhappy mistress saddled two mules and led them through the gate up to the vestibule of the palace, which opened upon a little street. He had many a time before accompanied Donna Olympia on some crazy errand. The others followed with the chair, laughing and cracking jokes.

Hurrying down the steps the madwoman ran against Ascanio, who, uneasy at hearing no further tidings, had come in person to find out what was going on.

" Has anything happened to Signora ? " he asked eagerly.

" Yes, a misfortune," she croaked hoarsely, like a flying raven, and springing upon her beast spurred it with crazy heels and disap- peared in the darkness.

Ascanio groped his way through the dark chambers until he reached Antiope's room, which was still lighted by the lamp Madonna Olympia had left standing there. As he looked around, the door of the house-chapel opened, and two happy spirits ascended from the depths. The strong-hearted man began to tremble. " Astorre, hast thou married her ? " he asked. The fatal word as it echoed and re-echoed through the lofty vault sounded like the last trump. "And hast Diana's ring on thy finger?"

Astorre wrenched it off and flung it away.

Ascanio flew to the open window through which the ring had vanished. "It has fallen into a crevice between the stones," said some one from the street below. Ascanio recognized turbans and helmets. They were the governor's body-guard who had begun their nightly round.

"One word with you Abu Mahommed," cried he, quickly resolved, to a white-haired old man who politely replied, "Thy wish is my command!" and with two other Saracens instantly disappeared in the gate-way to the palace.

Abu Mahommed al Tabib not only watched over the safety of the streets but likewise had entrance into all the houses in order to take under custody traitors to the Empire, or those whom the Governor regarded as such. Emperor Frederic had sent him as a present to his son-in-law the Tyrant, that he might organize for him a Saracen body-guard, and he had remained as their

chief in Padua. Abu Mahommed had a
fine presence and winning manners. He
sympathized with the grief of a family from
which he was obliged to take one of its
members to the prison, or the block, and
comforted the afflicted, in his broken Italian,
by quoting proverbs from the Arab poets.
I suspect that he owed his nickname, "al
Tabib" which means "the physician," even
if he may have possessed some chirurgical
knowledge, first and foremost to certain
ways that reminded one of a kind physician;
encouraging gestures, soothing words, as for
example, "it does not hurt," "it is quickly
over," with which the disciples of Galen are
accustomed to preface painful operations.
In short, Abu Mahommed handled his
tragical duty with tenderness and, at the time
of my story, was far from being a hated person-
ality in Padua, despite his severe and bitter
office. Later when the tyrant found a pleasure in torturing the bodies of men (a thing
which you cannot believe, Cangrande), Abu
Mahommed left him and returned to his
kind-hearted Emperor.

Upon the threshold of the chamber Abu

Mahommed motioned to his three attendants
to stop. The German who bore the torch, a
defiant-looking fellow, did not wait long
however. To-day, at the vesper hour he had
accompanied Germano to the palace of the
Vicedomini and the latter had said to him,
laughingly, "Leave me now, I am going to
espouse my dear sister Diana to the monk."
The German knew his commander's sister
and had a sort of quiet admiration for her
with her stately figure, and honest eyes.
When now he saw the monk, by whose side
he rode at mid-day, hand in hand with a
delicate little woman, who compared with the
magnificent stature of Diana, seemed like a
doll, he suspected breach of faith, flung his
burning torch angrily upon the stone floor,
from which one of the Saracens carefully
picked it up, and hurried off to acquaint
Germano with the monk's treason.

Ascanio, divining the German's intention,
begged Abu Mahommed to call him back,
but he refused. "He would not obey," he
said meekly, "and he is quite capable of
slaughtering two or three of my attendants.
In what other way can I serve you, Signor?

Shall I imprison these blushing young people?"

."Astorre, they will separate us," shrieked Antiope, and sought refuge in the arms of the monk. The crime at the altar, although committed with a guileless soul, had robbed her of her natural courage. The monk on the other hand, emboldened and inspired by his guilty act, took one step toward the Saracen, and snatched his sword from its sheath. "Carefully, boy, you might cut yourself!" said Abu Mahommed good-naturedly.

"Let me tell you Abu," explained Ascanio, "this frantic man is my friend, and was for many years the monk Astorre, whom you surely must have seen in the streets of Padua. His own father cheated him out of his cloister vows and betrothed him to a woman he did not love. A few hours ago he exchanged rings with her, and now, as you see him here, he is the husband of another."

"Fate," interposed the Saracen gently.

"And the betrayed one" continued Ascanio, "is Diana Pizziguerra, Germano's sister. You know Germano; he is trustful and confiding by nature, but when he finds that he has been deceived, the blood rushes to his eyes and he kills."

"Naturally," assented Abu Mahommed, "He is on his mother's side a German, and they are children of the truth."

"Advise me, Saracen! I know of but one recourse, perhaps a means of salvation, which is to bring the case before the Governor. Ezzelin shall judge. Meanwhile, let your people keep guard over the monk in his own strong castle. I hasten to my uncle. But you, Abu Mahommed, take this lady to the Countess Cunizza, sister of the governor, the pious and much-beloved Domina, who for several weeks has had her court here. Take the pretty sinner, I trust her to your gray hair!"

"You may," said Mahommed, as if to reassure him.

At this Antiope clung to the monk, crying even more piteously than at first. "They will separate me from you. Do not leave me Astorre, not for an hour, not for a moment, or I shall die!" The monk lifted his sword.

Ascanio, who abhorred all violence, turned appealingly to the Saracen. With fatherly eyes the old man gazed at the lovers. "Oh let the poor shades cling together," he said in a soft tone, "do not begrudge the poor loving butterflies this one hour," — either he was a philosopher and held life as an empty show, or he suspected that they would indeed be shades on the morrow through the condemnation of Ezzelin.

Ascanio, who never doubted the substantial reality of things, was fully alive to the second meaning, and, kind and tender hearted fellow as he was, hesitated to tear the loving ones asunder.

"Astorre," he asked, "do you know me?"

"You were my friend," answered the monk.

"And am so still, you have no truer."

"Oh, do not separate me from her," said the monk, in such an imploring tone that Ascanio could not withstand it.

"Well, then, remain together until you must appear before your judge." He then whispered something to Abu Mahommed.

The Saracen approached the monk and

gently took the sword away from him, loosening his grasp finger by finger, and dropped it back into its scabbard. Then he stepped to the window and beckoned to his troop. The Saracens immediately took possession of Madonna Olympia's chair which had been left in the vestibule and brought it to the door for Antiope.

Through a dark narrow court the hurried procession now moved onward. Antiope first, borne by four Saracens, at her side the monk and Ascanio, then the whole turbaned band, Abu Mahommed bringing up the rear.

They pursued their way across a small square, and passed a dimly-lighted church and as they were entering a dark lane on the other side of it, ran violently against a procession followed by an enormous crowd of people. A tumult arose. "Room for the Sposina," the people cried. Choir-boys brought out of the church long candles, whose flickering flames they protected with their hands. The dim yellow light revealed a litter and a bier. The Sposina was a young plebeian bride who had died suddenly; they were bearing her corpse to the grave.

Antiope sprang from her chair, and the assembled people recognized the monk, who threw his arms protectingly around her, while they knew he had been betrothed this very day to Diana Pizziguerra. Abu Mahommed, however, commanded order, and it was soon restored, so that without further adventure they reached the palace.

Astorre and Antiope were received by the servants with looks of astonishment. They quickly entered the door-way and vanished without bidding farewell even to Abu Mahommed and Ascanio. The latter wrapt himself in his cloak, and accompanied the Saracen a few steps further, as he made his nightly round of the castle where he was on guard, counting its gates, and measuring with his eyes the height of the walls.

" An eventful day," said Ascanio. " A blessed night," answered the Saracen looking at the star-sown heavens.

The eternal lights, whether ruling human fate or not, moved on according to their own silent laws, until Aurora with flaming torch kindled a new day, the last Astorre and Antiope were ever to see.

In the early morning hour, the tyrant and his nephew looked down through a little round window in his tower upon the square beneath. It was filled with an excited multitude, and the busy hum of voices rose like the surge of ocean-billows.

The news of the encounter of Antiope's chair with the bier yesterday evening, and the excitement it caused had flown through the city with the speed of lightning. All heads, waking or dreaming, were occupied with nothing but the monk and his wedding; — not only had he sacreligiously broken his vows to heaven, but now his earthly ones as well; he had betrayed his bride, flung his ring away, and with rashly-kindled passion wooed another, a fifteen year old maiden, just budding into life. The tyrant, who would countenance no illegal proceedings, ordered the house, in which the two sinners were concealed, to be guarded by his Saracens; he meant to-day to bring to judgment the misdeeds of the two aristocrats; — for the young Antiope was a Canossa; — to restore the chaste Diana to her rightful position, and, lest the virtue of his people should suffer through the bad example of their nobles, to throw the bloody heads of the misdoers out of the window.

The tyrant, while he fixed his eyes on the seething crowd below, listened to Ascanio's account of what happened yesterday. The love of the two young people did not move him at all, but the incident of the ring struck him as a new manifestation of Fate. " I blame you for not having torn them apart at once. I approve your having put them under arrest. The betrothal with Diana is legal. The Sacrament, forced by the sword, or bought with the purse, is null and void. The priest who allowed himself to be frightened or bribed, deserves the gallows, and if caught will swing. Once more, why did not you step between the untutored boy and the child? Why did you not wrench an ecstatic fool out of the arms of a poor bewildered maiden? You gave her to him! Now they are man and wife."

Ascanio, who, after a good night's sleep had regained his light-heartedness, concealed a smile. " Ha, Epicurean! " said Ezzelin reproachfully. But in a coaxing tone Ascanio answered, "It is done, my illustrious uncle, and now if you will only take the case into your powerful hands everything will be righted. I have summoned both parties. If you have the will, Ezzelin, by your firm judicious hand this knot is easily untied. Love is a spendthrift; and avarice knows not honor. The enamoured monk will gladly fling to the base miser, old Pizziguerra, whatever sum of money he desires. Germano will draw his sword; no doubt, you must bid him thrust it back into its scabbard. He is your man! He will gnash his teeth but he will obey."

"I ask myself," said Ezzelin, "whether I do right to defend the monk from the sword of Germano. Is Astorre to be allowed to live? Can he live, having flung aside the sandal of the monk, and trodden the newly-donned shoe of the knight in the mire resolving the *Cantus firmus* of the monastery into the yell of a vulgar street-song? I may do my best to lengthen out the existence of this vacillating, worthless man, but can I ward off his fate? If Astorre is destined to die by the hand of Germano I

may command the latter to lower his sword,
yet the former will run upon it. I know
this; I have experienced it;" and he fell to
brooding.

Ascanio turned his face away. He knew
a cruel history,

The tyrant had once besieged and taken
a castle where the rebels, who had held
out against him, were all condemned to the
sword. One of the soldiers was appointed
to execute this command. Among the first
to receive the death-stroke knelt a beautiful
boy, whose features attracted the tyrant.
Ezzelin detected in them a resemblance to
his own, and inquired of the youth his name
and origin. He proved to be the son of a
woman whom Ezzelin had loved and wronged
years before. He pardoned the condemned.
The boy, excited, urged on by his own curiosity, and perhaps by the envious taunts of
those who had lost their sons or relations by
this bloody sentence, did not rest until he
had solved the mystery of his preference.
He is said to have drawn the dagger
against his own mother and thus obliged her
to confess the wretched secret. The dis-

closure of his illegitimacy poisoned his young soul. He conspired anew against the tyrant, fell upon him in the street, and was cut down by the same soldier who had before lifted the sword to kill him, and now happened to be the first to come to Ezzelin's rescue.

Ezzelin, whilst reflecting on the fate of his son, dropped his head and covered his face with his right hand. Then he raised it slowly and asked, "But what is to become of Diana?"

Ascanio shrugged his shoulders. "Diana was born under an evil star," he said. "She has had to resign two husbands, one to the Brenta, the other to a more lovely woman; and added to all this her miserly father! She must retire into a convent, — what else remains for her?"

At this moment a tumult arose in the square below, — murmurs, threats, curses were heard on all sides; irritated individuals shouted and yelled, but just as the single voices seemed about to unite in the one hideous cry, "Death to the Monk!" the fury of the mob changed singularly, and only

a long-drawn note of admiration and amazement, and "Ah! Ah! how beautiful she is!"
passed from mouth to mouth. Through the
window the tyrant and Ascanio could
comfortably watch this scene. Saracens on
slender Arab steeds surrounded the monk
Astorre, and his young wife, both borne
along by mules. The new Vicedomini rode
veiled, but when the thousand hands of the
people were raised in violence to attack the
monk, her husband, she threw her arms passionately around him. The hasty movement
tore her veil. It was not alone the charm
of her face, nor the youthful beauty of her
figure, which had disarmed the crowd; but
the full play of her spirit, the unreserved
feeling, the living inspiration, which trans-
ported every one, as it had the monk the
day before, who now moved on like a triumphant victor with his spoils, fearing nothing, and
with the air of one who bore a charmed life.

Ezzelin observed this conquest of beauty
almost with contempt, but turned with
interest toward a second procession which
was entering the square from the other side.
Three nobles, accompanied like Astorre, by

a large number of people, were making their way through the crowd. Conspicuous among them rose the snow-white head of the old Pizziguerra, on his left Germano. The wrath of the soldier-knight yesterday had been terrible, when his German brought him the news of Astorre's treachery. He was rushing forward to take instant revenge when he was met and restrained by the Saracen who brought him the summons to appear at the palace of the governor early on the following morning. He was then obliged to tell his sister of the monk's crime, which he would have preferred to conceal from her until after he had avenged the wrong. She had received the tidings with perfect composure, and now rode on her father's right, the same as ever, save that her stately head was bowed one shade lower by the heavy thought it bore.

The crowd that a minute ago would have proclaimed with a sort of wrathful triumph the coming of the injured one to claim her rights, now, dazzled by the beauty of Antiope, comprehending, but at the same time forgiving the treachery of the monk, contented

themselves with sympathetic murmurs, such
as — "the poor soul, always unfortunate,
always sacrificed!"

The five now entered the bare hall where
the tyrant was sitting in a chair raised a few
steps above the ground. The contending
parties respectfully took their places opposite each other; here Pizziguerra and a
little at one side the grand form of Diana,
there the monk and Antiope with hands
locked together. Ascanio leaned against
the high chair of the tyrant, as if he would
take an impartial position between his two
old comrades.

"Signors," began Ezzelin, "I shall not
treat your case as a state affair, where breach
of faith is treason, and this treason a capital
offense, but simply as a family matter. In
fact the Pizziguerra, the Vicedomini and the
Canossa are of as noble blood as myself, only
the favor of his august majesty has made me
governor over these your lands." Ezzelin
bowed his head in recognition of the higher
power; he could not uncover it, for he was
accustomed to go bare-headed through all
kinds of wind and weather, except when

forced to don the warrior's helmet. "Thus we twelve noble families form a great household to which I belong in virtue of one of my maternal ancestors. But we are sadly reduced in numbers through the blind folly and wicked mutiny of some members against the highest worldly authority. If you sympathize with me we shall spare and preserve the few still belonging to us. On this ground I restrain the revenge of the Pizziguerra against Astorre Vicedomini, although I call it in its innermost nature a just one. If you" and he turned to the three Pizziguerra, "do not approve of my leniency, consider this one thing. I, Ezzelin da Romano, am the first and therefore the chief cause of all this misfortune. Had I not on a certain day, and at a certain hour, ridden along the banks of the Brenta, Diana would now be properly married, and this man still murmuring his breviary. Had I not ordered my Germans to muster on a certain day and at a certain hour Germano would not have given the monk such an untimely ride, and the ring on the hand of this lady beside him, rolled to her by his evil demon "—("by my

good genius" joyfully interposed the monk)
would have been drawn off her finger again.
Therefore Signors, help me to unravel and
smooth out this intricate matter, for, if you insist on stern justice I must first and foremost
condemn myself.

This extraordinary speech did not put the
old Pizziguerra out of countenance and when
the tyrant turning to him said, " My noble
lord you are the complainant," he replied
briefly, " Eccellenza, Astorre Vicedomini betrothed himself publicly and in the regular
form to my child Diana, and then without
Diana's having offended him in any way,
broke his engagement. This inexcusable,
illegal, sacriligious deed, weighs heavily, and
demands, if not blood, which your Grace
does not wish to shed, a heavy penalty," and
he made the gestures of a shopkeeper piling
weight upon weight into his scales.

" Without Diana's having offended him ? "
repeated the tyrant. " It seems to me she
did offend. Had she not an insane woman
before her? Yet Diana reviled and struck.
Diana gives way to violent passion when
she thinks her rights infringed."

Diana nodded and said, "You speak the truth, Ezzelin!"

"And this it was," continued the tyrant, "which turned Astorre's heart away from her, he saw in her a barbarian."

"No, my Prince," contradicted the monk, insulting the betrayed one afresh, "I never looked at Diana, I only saw the sweet face which received the blow, and my whole soul was moved to pity and love."

The tyrant shrugged his shoulders. "You see, Pizziguerra," he smiled, "the monk is like a maiden who for the first time has tasted strong wine and behaves accordingly. But we are old sober people; we must contrive some settlement of this affair."

Pizziguerra answered, "Much, Ezzelin, would I do to please you, because of your great service to Padua. Yet can the insulted honor of our house be propitiated otherwise than with the sword?" Thus speaking Diana's father made a stately flourish with his arm which somehow ended in a movement very like that of a man who holds out his hand to be filled.

"Astorre, make an offer!" said the governor with the double meaning, "either of your hand, or your money and lands."

"My Prince," and the monk now turned frankly and nobly to the tyrant, "if you call me unstable, or bereft of my senses, I cannot blame you, for a powerful God whom I denied, because I did not suspect his existence, has taken his revenge and completely over-powered me. Even now he drives me like a storm-wind whirling my mantle over my head. Must my happiness — oh, beggarly word! — must the highest boon of my life be paid for with my life? I accept it and find the price all too low. But if I may live, and live with her, I will not haggle," and he added with a blissful smile, "take my entire fortune, Pizziguerra?"

"My friend," pursued the tyrant, "I will assume the guardianship of this spendthrift-lover. Let me negotiate with you, Pizzi-guerra. You hear that he has given me full power to do so. What do you say to the mines of the Vicedomini?"

The old man preserved a decent silence, but his eyes which were near together glis-tened like two diamonds.

" Take my pearl fisheries also," cried Astorre, but Ascanio came gliding down the steps and closed his mouth with his hand.

" Noble Pizziguerra, take the mines," said Ezzelin persuasively, " I know the honor of your house is beyond everything and is not to be bought at any price, but I know like-wise that you are a good Paduan and will stretch a point for the peace of your city."

The old man remained obstinately silent.

" Take the mine he offers, and let him keep his own mine of joy!" urged Ezzelin, who enjoyed a play upon words.

" The mines and the fisheries?" asked the old man as if hearing with difficulty.

" The mines, I said, and nothing else. They yield many thousand pounds annually. If you should demand more, Pizziguerra, I should feel myself deceived in you and you would certainly expose yourself to the hate-ful suspicion of chaffering over your honor."

The old miser was afraid of the tyrant, and since he dared not demand any more, gulped down his vexation and extended to the monk his withered hand. " We must have it in writing," he said, " since life is uncertain."

He drew from his girdle-pocket a small account book and pencil, scratched with trembling fingers a rough draft of the title deed and gave it to the monk to sign. This done, he bowed before the governor and because of his feeble health begged to be excused, although one of the twelve, from attending the monk's marriage-feast.

Germano had stood beside his father burning with rage. Now he unfastened one of his iron gloves and would have flung it into the mónk's face had not a commanding gesture of the tyrant's bidden him halt.

"Son, will you break the public peace?" interposed the old Pizziguerra. "My word given, includes and guarantees yours. Obey or be cursed. I will disinherit you!" he threatened.

Germano laughed. "Attend to your own dirty bargains, father," he replied contemptuously. "Yet surely you, Ezzelin, Lord of Padua, will not hinder me. It is my manly right and a private affair. If I refuse obedience to the Emperor, and to thee, his governor, have me beheaded: but with your sense of justice you will not hinder me from

throttling this monk who has fooled and
deceived me and my sister. If falsehood is
to go unpunished who would wish to live?
This earth is a place too small for the monk
and me to inhabit together. He will understand this himself when he comes to his
senses."

"Germano,' said Ezzelin, "I am thy
commander-in-chief. Tomorrow the trumpet
may summon us to the battle-field. Thou
belongest not alone to thyself or to thy
family, but to the Empire."

Germano made no answer. He re-fastened
his glove. Then he exclaimed, "In old
times, among the blind heathen, there was
a god who avenged breaches of faith. I
don't think this has changed with the ringing of church bells. To Him I commit my
cause! and he ended by lifting his hands
fervently to heaven.

"Then it is in good hands," and Ezzelin
smiled. "This evening the wedding is to be
celebrated with masks in the Vicedomini
palace, according to custom. I give the
feast and invite you Germano and Diana.
Not in armor, Germano, with short sword!"

"Cruel," groaned the soldier. "Come, father, how can you longer make a spectacle of our disgrace?" And he dragged the old man away with him.

"And you Diana?" asked Ezzelin, as he saw that she alone and the newly-married pair were still before his judgement seat. "Do you not accompany your father and brother?" "If you will permit me," said she, "I have a word to say to this lady," and overlooking the monk, fastened her eyes upon Antiope.

Antiope, whose hand had all this time rested in that of the monk, followed the whole proceeding with deep interest, and though a passive spectator evinced a series of lively emotions. Now she blushed with a young wife's first love, then she turned pale with a feeling of guilt as she discovered under Ezzelin's smile and gracious words his real condemnation of them. One moment she exulted like a child escaping punishment, and the next showed a dawning consciousness of her dignity as the wife of the new Vicedomini. But when Diana addressed her she cast a shy inimical look at her powerful rival.

Diana, however, was not to be turned aside. "See here Antiope, my finger bears your husband's ring;" she stretched it out, " This you must not forget. I am not super-stitious as most people, but in your place I confess it would disturb my peace of mind. Deeply as you have sinned against me I will nevertheless be good and merciful to you. According to custom this evening your marriage is to be celebrated with masks. I shall appear to you. Come repentant and humbly to draw this ring yourself from my finger."

Antiope uttered a cry of fear and clung to her husband, where protected by his arms she said excitedly, " I am to humble myself, what do you bid me Astorre? My honor is thine, I am no longer aught but thy prop-erty, thy heart, thy breath of life, thy soul. If thou allow or command it, then —"

Astorre tenderly soothed his wife, and turning to Diana said, " She will do it. May her humility and mine propitiate thee. Be our guest this evening and remain friendly to my house." He next addressed Ezzelin respectfully thanking him for his judgment and his favor, bowed and led his wife away. But upon the threshold he stopped an instant to inquire of Diana, "In what costume will you appear amoug us to-night that we may recognize you and show you honor?"

She smiled contemptuously and again speaking to Antiope, "I shall come as that which I call myself and which I am. The untouched, the maidenly," she said proudly. Then she repeated, "Antiope remember, come humbly and repentant."

"You mean it honestly, Diana? You have no covert design? questioned the tyrant when the Pizziguerra was left alone with him.

"None," she replied, disdaining further protestation.

"And what will become of you, Diana?" he asked. "Ezzelin," she answered bitterly, "before this thy judgment-seat, my father has bartered away our honor and right to revenge for a few lumps of metal. I am not worthy to have the sun shine on me. The cell alone remains for such as I am!" And she left the hall.

"Most excellent uncle," said Ascanio

joyfully. You have united the happiest pair in Padua, and converted a tragic drama into a charming idyl, with which I shall enter-tain my children and grand-children at our hearth fire when I am a venerable old man."

" My nephew! composer of idyls!" said the tyrant with a dash of raillery as he stepped to the window to look down upon the square where the crowd still lingered in feverish curiosity. Ezzelin had given directions to have those leaving the palace before him let out by the back door.

" Paduans," he said in a powerful tone, (the multitude were silent as the desert) I have examined the matter. It was intricate and there was fault on both sides. I have pardoned it, for I am always inclined to mercy when the majesty of the Empire is not concerned. This evening the wedding of Astorre Vicedomini and Antiope Canossa will be celebrated, with masks. I, Ezzelin, give the feast and invite you all. May you enjoy it. I am the host. To you belong street and tavern. But let no one enter, or in any wise endanger the palace of the Vicedomini, else by my hand — and now return each of you quietly to his home if you love me."

An indistinct murmur arose, it rippled and ran. "How they love you!" joked Ascanio.

Dante paused for breath, then with rapid sentences concluded his story.

The trial being over at mid-day the tyrant rode forth to visit a remote castle which was in process of rebuilding. He desired and intended to return to Padua early in the evening that he might see Antiope humiliate herself before Diana.

Contrary to all will and foresight, however, he was detained. A Saracen came galloping after him into the court-yard of the castle, breathless and covered with dust, to deliver a letter by the Emperor's own hand which required immediate answer. The matter was of importance. A short time before, Ezzelin had fallen upon an Imperial stronghold at Ferrara, in the night, the commander of which, a Sicilian, his keen eye suspected of being a traitor. Ezzelin had taken the citadel and put the hypocritical Imperial governor in chains. Now the Hohenstaufen demanded the reason for this clever but daring infringement on his authority. With his left hand pressed upon his thinking brow Ezzelin's right glided swiftly over the parchment as his stylus went on from first to second and from second to third. He discussed radically, with his illustrious father-in-law, the aim and possibilities involved in a campaign at that moment impending, or at least planned. Thus the hours sped away and it was only when he remounted his horse that he knew from the aspect of the heavens — for the stars were all out in fullest brilliancy — that it would be impossible to reach Padua before midnight. Leaving his retinue far behind, like a spirit he flew over the nightly plain. But he chose his way and rode cautiously round a small ditch over which the bold horseman on any other day would have thought it play to leap; he would not risk the chance of a fall from the horse which might detain him. Again he spurred on his steed and the racer stretched himself out, but Padua's lights did not yet glimmer through the darkness.

Before the great city castle of the Vice-

domini, even as the twilight melted into the
dark of evening the intoxicated people had
assembled. Scenes of wanton, unbridled
mirth alternated with more innocent sport
on this not very large piazza. A wild passionate merriment, a species of bacchanalian
hilarity, seemed fermenting in the dense
crowd to which the youths from the High
School added an element of wit and derision.
The tumult was now interrupted by a long-
drawn-out Cantilene, or kind of litany, such
as our country-people used to sing. It was
a procession of peasants, old and young,
from one of the numerous villages belonging
to the Vicedomini. These poor people,
who, in their isolation, had heard nothing of
the monk's return to the world, but only
through uncertain rumor of the espousals of
the heir, had started before sunrise with the
customary wedding-gifts and after a long
day's travel over the dusty highway had just
reached their destination. They held together and wound their way slowly through
the seething mass of the people in the square;
here a curly-haired boy with golden honey-
comb, there a shy, proud maiden bearing

tenderly on her arms a bleating lamb, decked
out with ribbons.   All longed for a sight of
their new master.

Little by little they now disappeared in
the arched entrance, where to the right and
left the torches flaring· in the iron rings
contended with the last clear light of day.
Ascanio, usually so pleasant and friendly,
as manager of the feast, issued his commands
from the doorway, yelling and screaming in
a most excited manner.

From hour to hour the mischievous dis-
position of the people increased, and to such
a pitch, that when, at last, the distinguished
masqueraders appeared they were pushed
and jostled in every direction without the
slightest respect for their rank.   The torches
were snatched from the hands of their attendants and trodden out on the stone pavement,
the ladies separated from their manly escorts
and wantonly insulted, with no fear of a
dagger-stroke, such as on any other evening
would instantly have requited such audacity.

Especially one tall figure in the guise of a
Diana had to struggle against a dense ring
of low ecclesiastics and schoolboys.   A lean

haggard man was parading his mythological knowledge. " Thou art not Diana," he said in a nasal tone, " but quite another person. I recognize thee. Here sits thy little dove!" and he pointed to the silver crescent over the brow of the goddess. She, however, was not gracious like Aphrodite, but harsh like Artemis.

" Away swine," she said, vexed. " I am a true goddess, and abhor ecclesiastics." " Coo, Coo, Coo," said the man and in trying to touch her, uttered a frightful shriek and fell back, and moaning raised his hand. It was pierced through and through, and streaming with blood. The wrathful maiden had put her hand to the quiver at her back. She had stolen it from her brother and with one of his sharp finely cut arrows now chastised the loathsome hand.

Already, however, the attention of the mob was diverted by another spectacle quite as shocking, if not so bloody. The lowest and worst portion of the population of the town, pick-pockets, cut-throats, beggars and vaga-bonds of every description were yelling, whistling, dancing, joking and sneering in front and behind of a most grotesque-looking pair. A large, wild-looking woman, not without some remnants of beauty was arm in arm with a drunken monk in a tattered cowl. This was the cloister brother Serapion, who, spurred on by Astorre's example had escaped from his cell by night and for a week had been grovelling in the slums of the city. The crowd halted before a lighted corner of the palace and in a shrill voice and with gesticulations of a public crier the woman vociferated, "Know all men by these presents that soon the monk Astorre will slumber beside his wife Antiope." Hoarse extravagant laughter attended this announcement.

Gocciola's cap and bells now appeared at the open turret-window. "Good woman, be still!" said the fool in a whining voice, "you wound my educated feelings, and insult my sense of shame."

"Good fool," replied the impudent thing, "don't let this offend you. We give the proper name to what the aristocrats do. We put the labels on the apothecary's boxes."

"By my seven deadly sins," cried Serapion,

exultingly, "so we do; until midnight the marriage of my dear brother shall be proclaimed and sung out in all the squares of Padua. Forward! March! Hey-dey!" and he lifted his naked leg with the sandal, out of the heap of rags, which was all that remained of his soiled monastic dress.

These beastly pranks, added to the infuriated voices mingling in the crowd, beat like a storm upon the outer walls of the gloomy castle whose windows and apartments opened for the most part on the inner court.

In a quiet, secluded chamber Antiope was being dressed and adorned with flowers by her maids, Sotte and one other, whilst Astorre was receiving, at the top of the stairs, the endless swarm of guests.

"Sotte," whispered the bride to her servant who was braiding her hair, "you resemble me, and are just about my size, exchange clothes with me if you love me. Go and draw the ring from her finger repentant and humbly." Bow before the Pizziguerra, with arms crossed, like the veriest slave. Fall upon your knees. Throw yourself on the ground. Make a show of the most abject contrition, and pain. Only take from her the ring. I will reward you for this service royally. Take all the jewels I possess," she said imploringly. This temptation the vain Sotte could not withstand.

Astorre, who turned aside a moment from his duty as host to visit his beloved, found the two women exchanging dresses in the chamber. He instantly divined their intention "No, No, Antiope, you must not slip through it in this way," he said. "Our word must be kept. I ask it of your love. I command it!" and even as he hoped to soften the severe word with a kiss and a caress, he was torn away by Ascanio who hastened to explain that his peasants wished to offer him in person their gifts, and without delay, in order that they might start on their homeward journey in the cool of the night. When Antiope looked round in order to return her husband's kiss, she kissed the empty air.

She now hastily completed her toilet. Even the frivolous Sotte was frightened at the pallor of the face reflected in the glass. There was no sign of life in it save the terror in the eyes, and the glistening of the

firmly-set teeth. A red stripe, caused by
Diana's .blow, was visible upon her white
brow.

When at last arrayed, Astorre's wife rose
with beating pulse and throbbing temples,
and leaving her safe chamber hurried through
the halls to find Diana. She was urged on
by the excitement of both hope and fear.
She would fly back jubilantly, after she had
recovered the ring, to meet her husband
whom she wished to spare the sight of her
humiliation.

Soon among the masqueraders she distinguished the conspicuous figure of the Goddess
of the Chase, recognized her enemy and
followed, as with measured steps, she passed
through the main hall and retired into one
of the dimly-lighted small side rooms. It
seemed the Goddess desired not public
humiliation, but lowliness of heart.

Quickly Antiope bowed before Diana, and
forced her lips to utter, "Will you give me
the ring?" while she touched the powerful ⌐
finger.

"Humbly and penitently?" asked Diana.
"How else?" the unhappy child said fever-

ishly. "But you trifle with me; cruelly —
you have doubled up your finger!"

Whether Antiope imagined it, or whether
Diana really was trifling with her, a finger
is so easily curved! Cangrande, you have
accused me of injustice. I will not decide.

Enough! the Vicedomini raised her wil-
lowy figure and with flaming eyes fixed on
the severe face of Diana cried out, "Will
you torture a wife, maiden?" Then she
bent down again and tried with both hands
to pull the ring off her finger. Like a flash
of lightening a sharp pain went through her.
The avenging Diana, while surrendering to
her the left hand, had with the right drawn
an arrow from her quiver and plunged it
into Antiope's heart. She swayed first to
the left, then to the right, turned a little and
fell with the arrow still deep in her warm
flesh.

The monk, who, after bidding farewell to
his rustic guests, hastened back and eagerly
sought his wife, found her lifeless. With a
shriek of horror he threw himself upon her
and drew the arrow from her side, a stream
of blood followed. Astorre dropped sense-
less.

When he recovered from his swoon Germano was standing over him with crossed arms. "Are you the murderer?" asked the monk. "I murder no women," replied the other, sadly. "It is my sister who has demanded justice!"

Astorre groped for the arrow and found it. Springing up with a bound and grasping the long weapon with the bloody point he fell in blind rage upon his old playfellow. The warrior shuddered slightly before the ghastly figure in black with dishevelled hair and crimson-stained arrow in his hand.

He retreated a step. Drawing the short sword which in place of armour he was wearing and warding off the arrow with it, he said compassionately, "Go back to your cloister, Astorre, which you should never have left."

Suddenly he perceived the tyrant, who, followed by the entire company, was just entering the door opposite to them.

Ezzelin stretched out his right hand and commanded peace. Germano dutifully.lowered his weapon before his Chief. The infuriated monk seized the moment and plunged the arrow into the breast of the knight whose eyes were directed toward Ezzelin. But he also met his death pierced by the soldier's sword which had been raised again with the speed of lightning.

Germano sank to the ground. The monk, supported by Ascanio, made a few tottering steps toward his wife and laying himself by her side, mouth to mouth, expired.

The wedding-guests gathered about the husband and wife. Ezzelin gazed upon them for a moment then knelt upon one knee and closed first Antiope's and then Astorre's eyes. In the hush, through the open windows came the sound of revelry. Out of the darkness was heard the words, "Now slumbers the monk Astorre beside his wife Antiope," and a distant shout of laughter.

Dante arose. " I have paid for my place by the fire," he said, " and will now seek the blessing of sleep. May the God of Peace be with you!" He turned and stepped toward the door, which the page had opened. All eyes followed him, as by the dim light of a flickering torch, he slowly ascended the staircase.

THE END.

BELLES-LETTRES.

THACKERAY'S LONDON: His Haunts and the Scenes of his Novels. With two original portraits (etched and engraved); a facsimile of a page of the original manuscript of " The Newcomes;" together with several exquisitely engraved woodcuts. By WILLIAM H. RIDEING. 1 vol., square 12mo, cloth, full gilt, or in parchment covers in box, each $1.50.

" Mr. Rideing has made a delightful volume of these associations, quite in the spirit of Thackeray, and a volume for which countless readers of 'Vanity Fair' and ' The Newcomes' will thank him heartily." —*The Book-Buyer.*

THE TERRACE OF MON DÉSIR: A Novel of Russian Life. By the daughter of an American admiral, and wife of a Russian diplomate. 12mo, cloth, elegant, $1.25.

" It is to be hoped this is but the *avant garde* of many yet to come, and that in Madame de Meissner we may be proud to claim an American Henri Greville." — *Washington Sunday Herald.*

" A certain opulence in its swift panorama of bright scenes and high personages recalls somewhat ' Lothair.' " —*Boston Transcript.*

THE IMITATORS. A satire upon Boston by a Bostonian. In verse. 12mo, cloth, elegant, $1.25.

WHAT IS THEOSOPHY? By a Fellow of the Theosophical Society. A handbook of that " wisdom of the East " which is so much in vogue to-day. 12mo, cloth, 50 cents.

RICO AND WISELI. **Rico and Stineli, and how Rico Found a Home.** From the German of JOHANNA SPYRI, by LOUISE BROOKS. A companion to "Heidi." 12mo, 509 pp., cloth, elegant, $1.50.

A YEAR'S SONNETS. By LOUISE BROOKS. 1 vol., oblong quarto, printed in red and black upon hand-made paper, gilt-edged, and bound in white vellum, Japanese style. Limited edition. $2.00.

One of the choicest books in authorship and manufacture ever produced in Boston.

ARTHUR PENRHYN STANLEY, Dean of Westminster: HIS LIFE, WORK, AND TEACHINGS. By GRACE A. OLIVER. With fine etched portrait. Fourth edition. 1 vol., 12mo, half calf, $4.00; tree calf, $5.00; cloth, $1.50.

ANNOUCHKA. A Tale. By IVAN TURGENEF. 1 vol., 16mo, cloth, $1.50.

POEMS IN PROSE. By IVAN TURGENEF. With portrait. 1 vol., 12mo, cloth, gilt top, uncut edges, $1.25.

EVERY MAN HIS OWN POET; or, The Inspired Singer's Recipe Book. By W. H. MALLOCK, author of "New Republic," etc. Eleventh edition. 16mo, 25 cents.

THE ART OF FICTION. By WALTER BESANT and HENRY JAMES. Second edition. 1 vol., 16mo, cloth, 50 cents.

THE STORY OF IDA. By FRANCESCA. Edited, with Preface, by JOHN RUSKIN. With frontispiece by author. 16mo, limp cloth, red edges, 75 cents.

☞ *Any of the above works sent postpaid to any part of the United States or Canada on receipt of the price.*

CUPPLES & HURD, Publishers, Boston.